# A WILDER KIND OF LOVE

Rosaleena did not know what it was that made her open her eyes. Her ears were full of the gush of tumbling water so she could not hear any other sound.

Whatever it was, she suddenly sensed that she was under observation and not by Bridie.

She shielded her eyes and looked up.

There, high on the bluff above her, stood the figure of a man. Silhouetted against the sun, she could only see that he was tall, his shoulders broad and he wore a cape.

She cried out at the sight of the intruder and Bridie turned to look.

To Rosaleena's surprise, she showed no alarm, but merely raised her hand in greeting.

.The man waved back, then turned and disappeared.

Without a word of explanation, Bridie swam to the edge of the pool and Rosaleena followed.

She climbed out of the pool just as the sun dipped behind a cloud. In sudden shadow, no longer moving, she all at once felt very cold.

Teeth chattering, she watched as Bridie carelessly threw her dress on over her wet under-garments.

"W-who was that man?" she asked.

"A friend," replied Bridie casually.

She glanced at Rosaleena and laughed.

"Cold, are you? Ah, sure, you've no flesh on your bones at all!"

# THE BARBARA CARTLAND
# PINK COLLECTION

## Titles in this series

# A WILDER KIND OF LOVE

# BARBARA CARTLAND

Barbaracartland.com Ltd

# THE BARBARA CARTLAND PINK COLLECTION

Dame Barbara Cartland is still regarded as the most prolific bestselling author in the history of the world.

In her lifetime she was frequently in the Guinness Book of Records for writing more books than any other living author.

Her most amazing literary feat was to double her output from 10 books a year to over 20 books a year when she was 77 to meet the huge demand.

She went on writing continuously at this rate for 20 years and wrote her very last book at the age of 97, thus completing an incredible 400 books between the ages of 77 and 97.

Her publishers finally could not keep up with this phenomenal output, so at her death in 2000 she left behind an amazing 160 unpublished manuscripts, something that no other author has ever achieved.

Barbara's son, Ian McCorquodale, together with his daughter Iona, felt that it was their sacred duty to publish all these titles for Barbara's millions of admirers all over the world who so love her wonderful romances.

So in 2004 they started publishing the 160 brand new Barbara Cartlands as *The Barbara Cartland Pink Collection*, as Barbara's favourite colour was always pink – and yet more pink!

The Barbara Cartland Pink Collection is published monthly exclusively by Barbaracartland.com and the books are numbered in sequence from 1 to 160.

Enjoy receiving a brand new Barbara Cartland book each month by taking out an annual subscription to the Pink Collection, or purchase the books individually.

The Pink Collection is available from the Barbara Cartland website www.barbaracartland.com via mail order and through all good bookshops.

In addition Ian and Iona are proud to announce that The Barbara Cartland Pink Collection is now available in ebook format as from Valentine's Day 2011.

For more information, please contact us at:

Barbaracartland.com Ltd.
Camfield Place
Hatfield
Hertfordshire AL9 6JE
United Kingdom

Telephone: +44 (0)1707 642629
Fax: +44 (0)1707 663041
Email: info@barbaracartland.com

# THE LATE DAME BARBARA CARTLAND

Barbara Cartland who sadly died in May 2000 at the age of nearly 99 was the world's most famous romantic novelist who wrote 723 books in her lifetime with worldwide sales of over 1 billion copies and her books were translated into 36 different languages.

As well as romantic novels, she wrote historical biographies, 6 autobiographies, theatrical plays, books of advice on life, love, vitamins and cookery. She also found time to be a political speaker and television and radio personality.

She wrote her first book at the age of 21 and this was called *Jigsaw*. It became an immediate bestseller and sold 100,000 copies in hardback and was translated into 6 different languages. She wrote continuously throughout her life, writing bestsellers for an astonishing 76 years. Her books have always been immensely popular in the United States, where in 1976 her current books were at numbers 1 & 2 in the B. Dalton bestsellers list, a feat never achieved before or since by any author.

Barbara Cartland became a legend in her own lifetime and will be best remembered for her wonderful romantic novels, so loved by her millions of readers throughout the world.

Her books will always be treasured for their moral message, her pure and innocent heroines, her good looking and dashing heroes and above all her belief that the power of love is more important than anything else in everyone's life.

*"I have found that love can indeed be wild, impetuous and unpredictable. And I have known a few Irishmen as well as some Scotsmen in my lifetime and, take it from me, they are everything their reputation claims for them!"*

Barbara Cartland

# CHAPTER ONE
# 1818

The household at number 92 Portland Terrace was astir early.

Breakfast over, the whole establishment became a hive of activity.

Carpets were hung up in the yard to be beaten and silverware set out to be polished.

The tradesman's door was propped wide open for the constant relay of grocery boys and their packages and the larder stood ready for loins of pork, sides of beef, pink salmon on ice and pies of every description.

In the kitchen the cook had been toiling since early in the morning, baking pastries and, best of all, the cake!

It was the very day before Rosaleena Rosscullen's twenty-first birthday and a grand ball was planned.

Rosaleena was giddy with excitement.

Her dress was due to arrive tomorrow morning, but meanwhile she was to go shopping with her mother, Lady Rosscullen, for white leather gloves and an evening bag.

Once they had completed their purchases they were to take refreshments at Fortnum's Tea Rooms.

Seated at her dressing table and brushing out her luxurious golden hair, Rosaleena was enjoying the gentle breeze blowing in through the open window.

Her mother was reclined on a chaise, scanning the pages of a fashion magazine.

"Audley's has some pretty bonnets," she remarked. "Perhaps we might call in to take a look at them."

Rosaleena stopped brushing her hair, stared in the mirror and tried to picture a yellow bonnet on her head.

She was not vain, but she did have an appreciation for her appearance. Everyone said that she took after her mother, except for her brow, which was high and pale.

She had her mother's cupid's bow mouth as well as deep blue eyes and a pert chin.

"Mama?"

"Yes, dear?"

"About Audley's – "

"What about Audley's?"

Rosaleena regarded her patiently in the mirror.

"You remember – bonnets."

"Ah, yes! I thought we should take a look at some, didn't I?

Rosaleena frowned.

"I am not sure that Uncle Uriel will run to bonnets."

Lady Rosscullen flushed slightly.

"After tomorrow, my dearest, you will have a little more autonomy as regards your purse. Have you forgotten that you will come into your estate? Uncle Uriel will no longer be your Trustee.

"Not that," she now added hurriedly, "not that I am impugning his handling of all our finances. He has been a most diligent protector of our interests."

"Indeed, Mother," Rosaleena nodded politely and resumed her coiffure.

Lady Rosscullen appeared to register for the first time that her daughter was brushing her own hair.

She stood in indecision for a moment and then she came over to the dressing table.

"Shall I brush your hair for you, my dear?"

"Thank you, Mama."

She took the brush from her daughter and began to run it through the tresses, while looking at her.

'Such a beautiful girl,' she was thinking to herself. 'Such large shining eyes, such lovely porcelain skin. Such expressive features. There is little doubt but that she will make a very good marriage. Although it could never be as great a love match as my own!'

Noting a faint glimmer tears in her mother's eyes, Rosaleena guessed the direction of her thoughts.

"Mama?" she said gently.

"Oh, Rosaleena, I was just thinking – how perfect it would be if your father could be here to see what a lovely young woman you have become."

Rosaleena said nothing.

Her father had died in Ireland when she was less than a year old so she could not therefore be said to miss him, although she often wished that she had known him.

By all accounts, he was a kind and generous man. Not like – not like Uncle Uriel Reece.

Rosaleena felt immediately guilty, as if her mother could read her thoughts in turn.

She did not want her mother to know the truth – that she simply could not make herself love her step-uncle and Guardian or his son Oswald.

Discomforted by the feelings that always came to her whenever she thought about Uncle Uriel, Rosaleena distracted herself by turning to the window.

She gave a start when her eyes fell on the figure of a gentleman on the pavement opposite the house.

She could make out little about him, save that he had a tall and elegant frame, but one thing was clear.

His gaze was firmly trained on number 92.

Before she could dwell any more on this curious situation, he turned and beckoned to a waiting carriage.

Rosaleena craned her neck to watch him climb in.

"Do keep your head still!" scolded her mother.

"Sorry, Mama." Rosaleena dutifully stared straight ahead at the mirror.

She heard rather than saw the carriage depart as her mother finally drew back in satisfaction.

"There!" she cried. "Do you approve my efforts?"

Rosaleena regarded herself.

"It's perfect, Mama. I shall now ask you to do my hair every morning from now on!"

"Perhaps I shall be a lady's maid in my old age. Now – on with your boots, the carriage will be here soon."

Rosaleena hurried to be ready.

The morning's shopping passed swiftly and by half past eleven Rosaleena and her mother were taking their seats in Fortnum's Tea Rooms.

Fortnum's was an oasis of calm and tranquillity, only disturbed occasionally by the clatter of spoons and the chink of delicate china.

Idly letting her eyes run over the pretty room with its walls covered in blue chintz, Rosaleena became aware that she and her mother were now under scrutiny from a gentleman at an adjoining table.

She turned his way and blushed to meet his bright interested gaze.

Quickly she absorbed herself in re-arranging the tea set on her table, until the waiter arrived.

She soon forgot about her neighbour as she enjoyed playing hostess, although the silver teapot was almost too heavy for her grasp.

Then she and her mother fell into discussing their purchases and Rosaleena wondered whether there were any shops of note near the estate she was to inherit, Rosscullen House in Ireland.

Her mother laughed.

"Only Mrs. Jessop's quaint old store in Rosscullen village. You would have to travel to Dublin to purchase gloves as fine as those you bought today."

"Well, I daresay that I would not need such gloves if living in the country," Rosaleena mused.

Rosscullen House was often the poignant subject of conversation between herself and her mother.

Rosaleena longed to visit the land of her birth and her reputed beautiful estate, but then Lady Rosscullen was reluctant to return to where her husband had died.

"Excuse me."

Lady Rosscullen and Rosaleena were startled to be addressed by the gentleman at the adjoining table.

"Sir?" Lady Rosscullen addressed him civilly.

The gentleman inclined his head.

"My sincere apologies, madam. I could not help but overhear you mention Rosscullen House."

Lady Rosscullen looked uneasy.

"Indeed?"

"Indeed. You see, I myself was born in Ireland. I know the house and area you are speaking about well."

Lady Rosscullen shifted in her chair.

5

"Oh. How – lovely – "

His green eyes took in her obvious discomfit.

"Without wishing to intrude on your privacy, allow me to introduce myself. I am known as Colonel Joyce."

He now turned to Rosaleena who, eyes glued to his face, extended her hand.

His voice had entranced her with its soft lilt and musical cadence.

"I am Rosaleena Rosscullen," she said, not realising that she still held a spoon in the hand she proffered to him.

She was then cast into embarrassed turmoil when Colonel Joyce gently took hold of her hand, spoon and all, and managed to press it to his lips.

"Enchanted," he smiled.

Rosaleena blushed deeply.

Her mother now roused herself with just a hint of indignation.

"And I am – her mother. Lady Rosscullen."

Colonel Joyce turned and his eyes lingered on Lady Rosscullen and Rosaleena assumed that he was overcome by her mother's beauty.

"At your service, madam," he said at last.

The words were said in a way that they seemed to imply more than the usual courtesy.

'He really is a most intriguing gentleman,' thought Rosaleena and she cast an imploring glance at her mother.

Lady Rosscullen interpreted the glance correctly as, after a moment's hesitation, she graciously invited him to join their table.

"It is not often my daughter has the opportunity of discussing her homeland," she explained to Colonel Joyce.

The Colonel then replied that, alas, he himself had not visited his homeland for some years, as he had been stationed abroad for the duration of the Napoleonic War.

Hearing this, Rosaleena could barely contain her excitement. Since it was only three years since the Battle of Waterloo, then the Colonel must have fought under the Duke of Wellington!

In a tone of awe, she asked whether he had ever encountered Napoleon in the flesh.

Colonel Joyce replied that he had never seen him and then deftly changed the subject.

"I would far rather hear something about your own life, with your mother's permission, of course."

This Lady Rosscullen granted him, unused to such interest from a distinguished stranger.

Rosaleena proceeded with her history.

"I was born at Rosscullen House," she said, "in the year 1789, but I don't remember the place at all. My father died when I was only six months old and my mother and I were brought to England to live with Uncle Uriel."

She paused for a moment in surprise at the strange look that briefly crossed the Colonel's face. Before she could decipher it, he gave an encouraging smile.

"Go on, Miss Rosscullen."

She looked at her mother.

"Uncle Uriel is not my uncle by blood. He is my mother's step-brother, you see, and so he is really my step-uncle. He has a house in Portland Terrace and – that is where I grew up."

"How kind of him to take you under his wing," observed Colonel Joyce.

Rosaleena looked at him sharply.

Surely she had detected a dry tone to his remark?

But again he disarmed her with yet another smile.

"My father, shortly before he died, appointed Sir Uriel Reece as my Guardian," she continued.

Colonel Joyce regarded her with interest.

"Might I venture to enquire how your father, who must have been very young, met his death?"

Lady Rosscullen drew in her breath sharply, but Rosaleena affected not to hear.

She regarded the Colonel gravely.

"I know *when* my father died, but on the subject of *how* no one has ever cared to elaborate. We don't speak of him much at all."

Before the Colonel could respond, Lady Rosscullen put her hand to her bosom.

"It's too distressing a subject to be discussed," she whispered. "My heart broke forever when – when he died."

Without even turning her head, Rosaleena extracted a handkerchief from her sleeve and gave it to her mother.

"She will cry," she told the Colonel, across whose features danced a flicker of amusement.

"Rosaleena!" chided her mother, while pressing the handkerchief to her eyes. "You speak out of turn."

"I am sorry, Mama."

There was an awkward silence for a moment before the Colonel resumed,

"So, Miss Rosscullen, you and your mother live in London with your uncle?"

"And Oswald, when he is not away."

"Oswald?" The Colonel's eyes glinted.

"My Uncle Uriel's son. He is away at University so I don't see too much of him, for which I am sometimes grateful. I should feel sorry for him, I know, because his mother is dead, just like my father, but then Oswald can behave so badly. And Uncle Uriel never minds, although he is very forbidding with me."

"Oh, Rosaleena," sighed her mother reprovingly, handkerchief still in hand. "That's enough! Uncle Uriel has been so good to us. He has given us a home all these years and he is putting himself to much trouble arranging tomorrow's ball for you."

Rosaleena squirmed a little.

"I know he is. I am sorry, Mama."

Then, catching the Colonel's look of enquiry, she went on.

"Tomorrow is my twenty-first birthday and it is an important day for me because I come into my estate."

The Colonel bowed his head.

"My congratulations. I hope that your ball is a great success, Miss Rosscullen."

She turned in sudden excitement to her mother,

"Mama? Would it not be a grand idea to invite the Colonel to my ball?"

Lady Rosscullen appeared to flail for a response.

"I see no reason why not," she said at last, although her face suggested she wished she could find a hundred.

Rosaleena smiled at the Colonel happily.

"Please say you will accept!"

The Colonel, although he had clearly noted Lady Rosscullen's reluctance, inclined his head in assent.

"I should be delighted. I am at *Buswell's Hotel* in Covent Garden, if you care to send a formal invitation."

Eyes low, Rosaleena hugged to herself the thought that she had invited a guest to her ball of her very own choosing, not one approved beforehand by her Uncle Uriel.

On the way back, Rosaleena thought about her ball.

She had been taught at home by a Governess and so knew very few people of her own age, apart from Oswald.

The ball therefore would be composed of friends of her mother's and Sir Uriel's with their various offspring.

Amongst them would be Lady Fonders' daughter, Lalage, Rosaleena's only close confidante.

Lalage was a somewhat imperious young lady and her interest in Rosaleena blew hot and cold, according to whether she had an admirer in tow or not.

Still, thought Rosaleena, with a certain satisfaction, she would not have anyone as intriguing as Colonel Joyce.

The prospect of the ball tomorrow had now become even more delicious, the only flaw was that Oswald would be there, taking time off from his studies.

Thoughts of the son returned her to thoughts of the father. She suddenly faltered as she imagined Uncle Uriel vetoing her invitation to Colonel Joyce.

"Mama?"

"Yes, Rosaleena?"

"I think I would like the Colonel to be something of a secret for now."

"A secret?"

"Yes. I will not tell Uncle Uriel of the invitation and the Colonel's appearance will be a surprise, a pleasant one, I hope. Uncle Uriel is always saying that he has fond memories of Rosscullen House, despite – despite – "

"Despite the unfortunate circumstances that ended his stay there?" Lady Rosscullen finished for her.

Not wishing to upset her once again, Rosaleena fell silent.

"I consider the invitation to have been a somewhat rash move," continued her mother after a moment. "We know nothing about this Colonel Joyce. And I should not like to offend your uncle since he has been so good to us."

"Well, we cannot uninvite the Colonel, Mama!"

Rosaleena regarded her in silent reproof before a sudden glint of mischief appeared in her eyes.

"Mama," she said with affected solemnity, "did you not notice how the poor Colonel barely took his eyes from your face? He was just lost in admiration."

Lady Rosscullen looked suitably shocked.

"Rosaleena! I must cancel your subscription to the travelling library. All those new novels are putting ideas into your head!"

Rosaleena suppressed a giggle.

"If my views were truly influenced by my reading, I should have claimed the Colonel's admiration for myself. As it is, he is way too old for me, as he must be over thirty years of age at least!

"Although," and here her brow wrinkled a little, "I have to admit he had a most distinguished air. Did you not think so, Mama?"

Lady Rosscullen frowned.

"There was indeed something – familiar about that gentleman. Although I cannot place him at all – "

A few minutes later, the carriage then turned into Portland Terrace and drew up outside number 92.

The first thing Rosaleena did was rush to her room, where she wrote out an invitation for the Colonel and sent her maid out to catch the early afternoon post.

*

The next morning the dressmaker, Madame Fillon, arrived with Rosaleena's ballgown.

Rosaleena could not resist telling her all about the Colonel and how he had fought under Wellington.

Madame Fillon, about to open the box containing the ballgown, looked up with a twinkle,

"Supposing then he did not fight under your Mr. Wellington!"

Rosaleena frowned.

"What do you mean?"

"In 1798 there was a rebellion in Ireland against ze English. When it failed, many Irish rebels fled to France, because France helped zem in their struggle. And when Napoleon came in, many of these Irish rebels, zey fight for him! Zis Mr. Joyce, maybe he was in ze *French* Army!"

Rosaleena did not take her seriously. She could not for one second imagine that the Colonel was in the French and not the English Army.

She did, however, brood on the fact that this was the first time she had heard details of the 1798 rebellion.

Her mother always became very upset if the subject was raised and Rosaleena surmised that this was because it was in this self-same rebellion that her father had died.

"Mam'selle Rosaleena?"

Rosaleena shook herself.

"What is it, Madame Fillon?"

"You do not want to see zis dress?"

As Madame Fillon lifted the ballgown from its box, Rosaleena forgot about armies and rebellions and Colonels.

"Oh!" she breathed. "It's so beautiful."

It was indeed a vision of white silk and organza, trimmed with rose-coloured lace, the skirt billowing out as delicately as a butterfly's wings.

Lady Rosscullen then came in to see the gown.

Madame Fillon stood back, pins in mouth, ready to tackle any last minute problem. It was agreed that there were none and Rosaleena removed the dress and watched as it was laid carefully in a trunk amid scented tissue.

Once her mother and Madame had gone, Rosaleena stood before the pier glass in her petticoat and bodice.

She surveyed herself with as critical an eye as she could muster.

She was so trim with a tiny waist, slim ankles and dainty feet. And with that snow-white gown on, surely she would turn a few heads at the ball?

If there are any heads to turn, she reminded herself quickly. It was unlikely that there would be many eligible young men. Uncle Uriel hardly knew any and Oswald had refused to invite his friends as they were bored with balls.

There would, of course, be Colonel Joyce.

His rich lilting voice and those emerald green eyes contrived to haunt her. What a pity he was so very much older than herself –

*

The hour of the ball arrived at last.

Rosaleena descended the stairs to the large entrance hall in a kind of trance with her mother following proudly.

In the hall Sir Uriel turned to watch her descent and with him was Oswald just arrived from his University.

"Why, see just how beautiful your cousin is," said Sir Uriel loudly, attempting to rouse his son's interest.

Oswald glanced up as she reached the last step.

"You look splendid, cousin," he muttered.

He waited for a sign of approval from his father and, receiving none, seemed to remember himself,

"I hope you will reserve the first dance for me."

"With pleasure," consented Rosaleena loftily.

Oswald, duty now done as far as he was concerned, excused himself and wandered off to the ballroom.

Meanwhile, the sound of the first carriage drawing up outside reached Rosaleena's ears and along with her mother and uncle, she greeted the guests as they arrived.

Lord this and Lady that, the Reverend and Mrs. So-and-So, Admiral Who and Master What – the faces bobbed before her one after the other.

Only when Lalage Fonders arrived did she relax.

Lalage bustled forward, dressed in crimson with a Spanish mantilla around her shoulders.

"My mother sends her apologies but she is fearfully indisposed. She hopes you will pay her a visit soon, Lady Rosscullen, when she feels sure that she will be recovered enough to give Rosaleena her present. Oh, Rosaleena – !"

Lalage paused in her prattle to examine her friend.

"What a picture you are, to be sure!"

"Thank you for your compliment, Lalage."

"Compliment, nonsense! It's the living truth. Sir Uriel, Lady Roscullen, will you permit Rosaleena to come with me now, please? I do so want to hear all about her plans for the evening."

"Plans – I have no plans," Rosaleena protested, as she was dragged away by a determined Lalage.

Hearing the doorknocker sound on the front door, she twisted her head round to see if it might be Colonel Joyce, but it was only Alderman Crackshaw.

Once inside the ballroom, Lalage released her.

"I reckoned you had had quite enough of all that formal business," she confided merrily to Rosaleena.

"I certainly wished that I had more friends of my own to greet," said Rosaleena wistfully.

Lalage squeezed her arm.

"That uncle of yours has kept you cooped up like a chicken! Anyone would think he did not want you to meet people of your own age. Or at least young gentlemen."

Rosaleena glanced at her friend.

"Is that how it seems?"

"Oh, yes," said Lalage airily. "I mean – this is the very first ball he has thrown for you. And he is always inventing an excuse to prevent you attending mine, where you would meet all kinds of eligible fellows. I think he has his own plans for you!"

Rosaleena looked nervous.

"You do?"

"I do."

Lalage gestured with her head in the direction of Oswald, who was lurking by the fire, drink in hand.

Rosaleena's eyes widened.

"Oswald? You cannot mean it, Lalage."

"What could be better? Keeping the money in the family. And Oswald is not a complete frog, you know."

Rosaleena gave a giggle.

"I suppose he isn't."

"I grant he is not as handsome as Lord Bellam's son, Henry, who seems to be quite smitten with me. But – Oswald has a certain – *je ne sais quoi.*"

Rosaleena turned and examined Oswald, as if to determine what that *je ne sais quoi* might be.

She had to admit that, although he was not tall, he had a solid enough build and, while not handsome, he had an acceptable regularity of feature.

If only his expression was more genial, Rosaleena decided, he would indeed pass muster. If that was what '*je ne sais quoi* signified.

She wondered what Lalage would make of Colonel Joyce – if he ever arrived!

"Well?" demanded Lalage.

Rosaleena shrugged.

"I can see that Oswald is not without attraction, but I cannot reconcile myself to his – sulky air. And he can be a bully too."

"Nonsense! A domineering man is no bad thing."

Lalage gave Rosaleena a nudge in the ribs that quite startled her.

"He is making his way towards us, Rosaleena," she whispered. "Do you think it's you or me he will ask to dance?"

"Me," replied Rosaleena. "I pledged him the first."

Oswald had taken his cue from the musicians, who were tuning their instruments as he offered his arm to her.

Lalage raised her eyebrows as Rosaleena accepted Oswald's arm and then moved onto the dance floor as the musicians struck up and a lively waltz began.

"I am not that much interested in this sort of thing," noted Oswald. "I wish we had started with a little supper."

Rosaleena had no answer to this as her gaze drifted towards the door.

Where was Colonel Joyce?

"Are you listening, cousin?"

"I-I am sorry, Oswald."

"I was saying," sniffed Oswald, "that my father has suggested that you and I should become better acquainted."

"How better acquainted could we really become," Rosaleena asked wonderingly. "We have been members of the same household for many years?"

"I was not here all that often?" countered Oswald. "I was at school abroad in Switzerland. Rotten cold place it was too. Then I have been at University. That's all over now and Father has other plans for me."

"He does?" Rosaleena was bemused.

"Well, plans for *us*, should I say!"

"Us?" Rosaleena froze.

"Yes, us. Why have you stopped dancing? Come on, the waltz isn't finished yet."

She resumed the dance in a more mechanical way.

"What do you mean – plans for us?" she asked.

"Just plans," replied Oswald crossly. "And we had better go along with them if we are to keep the peace. But I will tell you about them later. Don't want you taking off like a frightened rabbit."

The music stopped and she stepped away from him.

"I think – I would like to sit out the next dance," she said faintly.

"Please yourself. I want to sneak into the supper room anyway. I'm starving."

Oswald led her back to Lalage and disappeared.

"You cannot imagine how unpalatable that was," began Rosaleena to her friend, but she faltered as she saw Lalage's attention shift towards the door.

"Who can that most distinguished gentleman be?" Lalage exclaimed.

Rosaleena turned and her heart skipped a beat.

There at the door, dressed in a dark green velveteen jacket, stood the man she had been waiting for all evening.

Colonel Joyce!

# CHAPTER TWO

Rosaleena reached the door at the same time as Sir Uriel and Lady Rosscullen, who then shot her a somewhat nervous look.

"Uncle Uriel," said Rosaleena, a little too brightly. "Allow me to introduce Colonel Joyce. Mama and I had the good fortune to become acquainted with him over tea at Fortnum's and I – invited him to my ball."

Sir Uriel looked furious, but he managed to give the Colonel a curt bow.

"You must surely have made quite an impression, Colonel, to be so honoured."

"I cannot answer for the impression I made, sir, but an honour it certainly is," the Colonel returned politely.

Rosaleena looked anxiously from one to the other.

"Uncle Uriel – I was sure you would enjoy meeting the Colonel, because – he hails from Ireland. In fact he knows Rosscullen well."

Rosaleena was disturbed to see Sir Uriel clench his fist at his side before responding,

"Indeed?"

"Indeed," nodded the Colonel. "And Rosscullen is a marvellous part of the country. Such haunting beauty."

Sir Uriel's lip curled.

"I am not a man, Colonel, to be haunted by beauty. Or by anything else for that matter."

"No doubt there is advantage to be gained by such a position," replied the Colonel coolly.

'Perhaps Mama was right,' thought Rosaleena with a sinking heart. 'And I should not have invited the Colonel without my uncle's permission.'

It was Lalage Fonders who then appeared.

"Do please introduce me to your friend," came her voice and she turned to see Lalage gazing at the Colonel.

"Oh! Miss Fonders!" Sir Uriel looked relieved. "This is Colonel Joyce. My niece met him at Fortnum's and I am sure he will be pleased to partner you in a dance."

Colonel Joyce barely blinked.

"It will be my pleasure," he said, extending his arm.

Lalage took it, giving a happy glance to Rosaleena.

As the swept off, Sir Uriel then turned to his niece.

"In future," he growled, "please refer to me before you invite anyone who you do not know to this house and remember that you are now a young lady of fortune."

"Yes, Uncle," replied Rosaleena meekly. "But the Colonel did not know of my fortune when he first engaged us – in conversation."

"But it is a fortune-hunter's business to search for quarry," snapped Sir Uriel.

Turning, he glared at Lady Rosscullen.

"And you, madam, should be more careful of your charge!"

Rosaleena's eyes now sought out Colonel Joyce on the dance floor. She had thought him to be 'too old', but, looking at him now, she had to admit that he was the most graceful gentleman in the room.

Lalage Fonders certainly thought so too as she was quite obviously hanging on his every word.

There were three more sets to be danced before supper and Lalage monopolised the Colonel for every one.

Rosaleena danced twice with Alderman Crackshaw and then with Sir Uriel.

As she circled the floor, she continually sought the Colonel's gaze, but only the once did their eyes meet over Lalage's shoulder.

Oswald reappeared to lead his cousin in to supper.

All through the meal she craned her head to watch the Colonel and Lalage. The Colonel was far too attentive to his companion for Rosaleena's liking.

After supper dancing started again and Rosaleena hoped that the Colonel would now at last approach her, but Lalage hurried him back onto the floor.

'It should be *me* in his arms,' Rosaleena told herself miserably.

Now the very sight of his head inclined towards his partner, the sight of his hand laid on the small of Lalage's back, seemed to shake her slight frame to its foundations.

This must be jealousy she mused with amazement. An emotion she had read about, but never experienced.

An emotion that she knew rendered people mad or drove them to – to kill!

She was not even sure at that very moment that he remembered her existence.

"You are not dancing?" a voice said in her ear.

She had been so immersed in her daydream that she had not heard the music end!

"C-Colonel?"

Colonel Joyce smiled ruefully.

"You are unsure? You have forgotten me already?"

"Oh, no!" replied Rosaleena hurriedly. "I have not forgotten you! I was – daydreaming. I do that often."

"And this particular daydream, was it of a pleasant nature?" enquired the Colonel.

Rosaleena's blush deepened and she was sure that the Colonel would guess her secret thoughts.

"Oh no, very mediocre," she said lamely. "Did you – were you taken by my good friend, Lalage? She is very beautiful, isn't she?"

"Very," agreed the Colonel solemnly. "I daresay she breaks hearts as easily as a cook breaks eggs!"

Rosaleena lowered her head.

"Well, at any rate – I hope that you are enjoying the ball," she whispered.

There was a silence and then, before she could even think to resist, the Colonel lifted her face to his.

"I would enjoy it even more," he said quietly, "if you consented to dance with me."

Rosaleena barely heard him.

Her cheeks burned beneath his grip, her blood rose, pulsating to the surface of her skin.

She trembled as she saw how the Colonel's pupils held a light at their centre like a flame in darkness. What was the meaning of that flame? Did it burn for her?

"Well?" she heard him demand.

Rosaleena could only nod her acquiescence. With a half-smile, the Colonel released her. He then extended his arm and she obediently placed her hand on it.

As she moved in a trance beside him, she heard the violins start up again.

She thought that she was now floating on a cloud of happiness, when an unwelcome voice broke in on her.

"I say, wha's this fella doing, mushcling in on my dance?"

It was Oswald, straddling the way before them. His hair hung over his face and his gait unsteady.

Rosaleena, roused from her state of near delirium, shrank back as she noted his condition.

"Oswald," she said faintly, "this – this is Colonel Joyce. Colonel, this is my step-cousin, Oswald."

He regarded Oswald, his eyes suddenly steely.

He tried a polite bow, but almost lost his footing.

"The devil!" he muttered angrily. "Roshaleena – give me your arm, do. For a turn about the floor."

Rosaleena protested,

"I did not promise every dance to you, Oswald. Only the first."

"Thash not how I undershtood it," returned Oswald.

Turning towards the Colonel, he pressed his fingers against his chest.

"Thing is, old fellow, the evening's mine in more ways than one."

Brusquely, the Colonel took Oswald's fingers and crushed them tight.

"And this dance, young fellow, is mine. I am not inclined to forego it."

Oswald winced in pain and his bravura was rapidly vanishing.

"All right, if you insist. Just let go, will you?"

The Colonel opened his fist and Oswald gingerly drew out his fingers.

He then led a pale and rather subdued Rosaleena onto the floor, Oswald's gaze following them sullenly.

"I think Oswald – has imbibed a little too much champagne," she tried to explain, but the Colonel stopped and pressed his hand to her lips.

"I forbid you to waste a second on that fellow," he said gently. "This dance is just for you and me alone. No ghosts allowed."

"G-ghosts?"

Her brow puckered, but only for a moment, as he took her in his arms and swept her away.

Oswald was forgotten, Uncle Uriel was forgotten, Lalage was forgotten.

The Colonel waltzed Rosaleena into a world that seemed fine as crystal and as delicate as the dew-drenched petals of a rose at dawn.

Her partner's manly form excited her in a way she could not fathom as she was inexperienced in such matters.

He exuded health, he was strong, his hand about her waist was firm yet tender. He brought his face close and his breath stirred her hair.

Eyes closed, she imagined his lips brushing hers.

She felt weightless, as if her feet left the ground.

'I feel – like a bird on the wing,' she sighed happily to herself and the Colonel heard.

"A dove," he murmured huskily. "Soft and gentle and pale as snow."

She heard his words in wonder. Did he too feel as if the room vanished, as if he and she were dancing on air?

Too soon, too soon, the dance ended.

Her breath short and her breast heaving, Rosaleena shuddered happily as he raised her hand to his lips.

A summons from behind came as a blow on her ear.

"Rosaleena!"

She spun round and flinched to see her uncle there, his brow grim.

"Niece, I hear you have been somewhat ungracious to my son," Sir Uriel remarked darkly.

"Why Uncle, no – I had simply agreed to dance with the Colonel and Oswald misunderstood – "

Sir Uriel's eyes flicked to the Colonel, who had let go of Rosaleena's hand and stood still with the watchful attention of an animal sensing danger.

"Be that as it may, niece," Sir Uriel said, "it is time for you to pay attention to your other guests. I am sure the Colonel will relinquish you now he has had his dance."

The Colonel's eyes were hooded.

"I will do only what the lady desires," he said.

Rosaleena threw him a grateful look.

What she desired was to rush back into his arms, to dance again with her breast crushed to his, but she was too well-schooled to neglect what she knew to be her duties.

"You are right to remind me," she addressed Sir Uriel in a low voice.

Turning, she curtseyed to her erstwhile partner.

"Colonel, you will excuse me, won't you?"

She could not read the Colonel's expression as he inclined his head.

"Of course, Miss Rosaleena."

She moved away, Sir Uriel remaining at her heels until he was sure that she had obeyed his command.

She circled amongst the guests politely, her mind elsewhere with the Colonel. She only came to her senses when she was waylaid by an exhilarated Lalage.

"I saw you dancing with the Colonel, Rosaleena. No doubt he asked you about me. I have made a conquest there, I can tell. So un-English, isn't he? Expresses his emotions so freely. I have invited him to lunch tomorrow to meet my Mama."

"I thought that your mother was indisposed."

The idea of Lalage having the Colonel to herself for an afternoon was sheer horror.

"I can play hostess if Mama is not recovered."

"And – has the Colonel accepted your invitation?"

"He has," Lalage smirked.

Rosaleena gave a forced smile and moved away. She wondered quite what emotion it was that the Colonel had expressed so freely to her friend. Had he called Lalage a dove – *soft and gentle and pale as snow*?

Too unsettled to continue with the Social niceties, Rosaleena slipped away. Heavy of heart, she made her way to the door that led into the garden.

"Ah, got you at last!"

Oswald caught at her dress from where he sat half-hidden by a fern.

Rosaleena frowned.

"Oswald, let go. I am on my way to the garden."

"To meet that Irish fellow, I suppose. Well – you shan't. Sit – here!"

With a tug, Oswald forced her down beside him.

"There's something I *have* to say to you."

"What is it?" asked Rosaleena impatiently.

"I am not going to go about it like a beater without a dog," said Oswald pompously. "The thing is, I am to ask you to marry me. There. It's done. What will you say?"

She was speechless as he regarded her blearily.

"What's your mouth open like that for? I'll stop it up, if you like."

To Rosaleena's horror, he then lunged towards her. One hand clutching the back of her head, he then pressed his lips greedily to hers, his sparse beard pricking her face.

She struggled in his grip and managed to wrench her face from his.

"How dare you!" she cried and pushed him so hard that he slid from the seat.

Not waiting to register his enraged howl, she rushed into the garden, stumbling into the path of Colonel Joyce.

"Miss Rosscullen!"

With astonishment he took in her dishevelled gown, the tears spilling onto her cheeks.

"What has happened?"

"Colonel!"

With a wild impulse she then fell against him and between sobs, blurted out the source of her distress.

His arms tightened about her as he listened.

"By Heaven, he will pay for his conduct," she heard him growl.

"No, sir," came an unwelcome voice. "It is you who will pay for yours!"

She turned her head from the Colonel's breast and there, his form dark and threatening as he advanced, was her uncle, Sir Uriel Reece.

"What is the meaning of your behaviour, sir?" he spat at Colonel Joyce.

"*My* behaviour?" replied the Colonel. "Sir, perhaps you are unaware that your niece has been grossly insulted by your son."

"It is I who have been insulted," fumed Sir Uriel. "From the moment you arrived under my roof you have attempted to seduce my niece away from her duties and away from the hitherto welcome attentions of my son."

Rosaleena gasped as he regarded Sir Uriel coldly.

"I most certainly don't believe that Miss Rosscullen ever welcomed the attentions of your son!"

"If not, it's because you have been using your Irish charm on her!" retorted Sir Uriel. "My son made an honest proposal to my niece and she will give it due consideration without your interference. After all the proposal was made with my consent as well as her mother's."

"M-my mother gave her consent?" she stammered.

So stunned was she by this revelation that she did not resist him when Sir Uriel grasped her arm ostensibly to steer her from the Colonel's reach.

"This young lady is my Ward, Colonel Joyce," he snarled. "You have no rights here and you are no longer welcome in my house. Please order your carriage or I shall have you thrown out."

The Colonel made an angry move, but Rosaleena threw him a look of such desolation that he fell back.

"Remember – I am always at your service," he said with great intensity before Sir Uriel hauled her away.

Rosaleena stumbled miserably alongside her uncle and he said nothing to her until they were inside the house.

"The ball is over for you," he snapped. "Go to your room. I will make your excuses to your guests."

Heavy-hearted, Rosaleena made her way upstairs.

She went straight to her window and was in time to catch the Colonel leaving. Her eyes devoured his figure as he stood pulling on his gloves forcefully.

He glanced up as his carriage drew alongside the kerb, but did not detect her in the darkened window.

Barely had he put one foot on the carriage step than a figure rushed out of the house behind him.

It was Lalage. Rosaleena heard her friend entreat the Colonel to take her home.

The Colonel did not hesitate, but handed Lalage in, before climbing up after her.

Rosaleena watched the carriage go. It was almost out of sight when she gave a sudden start.

Had she not seen that vehicle before?

She opened the window and leaned out to stare at it, but it had already rounded the corner.

"Rosaleena, what have you done?" her mother said behind her. "You have upset your uncle and me."

"And you have upset me so, Mama!" she reposted with a frown. "Could you not have discussed this proposal with me – before you agreed to it?"

Lady Rosscullen reddened.

"I thought it would be a pleasant surprise on your birthday."

"Mama!" Rosaleena exclaimed in shock. "Surely you know how I feel about Oswald? I have never had the slightest romantic interest in him."

"Oh, all this romance! Such notions you have. A marriage to Oswald would be very politic. Sir Uriel could continue to look after your money. And Oswald is – "

"An ass!" parried Rosaleena grimly.

Lady Rosscullen sank into an armchair.

"Well – at least he is an *English* ass, my sweet."

"How can you say such a thing, Mama, when you yourself married an Irishman?"

Lady Rosscullen's fingers plucked at her skirt.

"Your father was Anglo-Irish, and besides, he was exceptional. Irishmen are always wild and unpredictable. They can never, never be trusted!"

Rosaleena had not heard her mother speak in such a way before about her late husband's countrymen.

"You surely cannot believe Colonel Joyce – to be such a man as you describe," she said in a low voice.

Lady Rosscullen dabbed at her eyes.

"I make no exceptions, my dear," she said. "Please do try to look on Oswald in a more kindly light. I should so hate your uncle to be thwarted."

"Oh, so that is what this about," rejoined Rosaleena scornfully. "Pleasing Uncle Uriel."

Lady Rosscullen rose, trembling.

"I think that entrusting your future to the hands of someone who has concerned himself with your past is the best option for a – a fatherless girl. Heaven knows I don't feel equipped to make all the right decisions. Now I will leave you to reflect about the consequences of your ill-considered behaviour this evening. Let's hope that Oswald has not been discouraged for ever."

"Oh, let's hope he has," muttered Rosaleena under her breath as her mother swept from the room.

Her sense of defiance did not last long. Left alone, she could not but ponder on her feelings for a man who, since he was Irish, her mother must instinctively mistrust.

She had no illusions about tomorrow. Uncle Uriel would even now be composing a long boring lecture on her ingratitude to him and his son.

She had almost tasted the Colonel's lips and she had known what it was to swoon against his breast. How could she ever invite the embrace of Oswald after that?

She lay awake that night, staring into the dark.

She wished she did not keep thinking of Lalage, riding home in the Colonel's carriage – the one that she was certain she had seen before.

*

She went into breakfast tremulously the next day.

Sir Uriel glanced grimly at her over his coffee cup, but to her surprise he did not launch into a diatribe.

Her mother smiled a little wanly at her as she took her seat and Oswald was nowhere to be seen.

Sir Uriel cleared his throat.

"I must apologise for my son," he began.

Rosaleena looked up in surprise.

"Oswald is definitely not used to such a quantity of champagne," her uncle continued, "and he admits that he may have behaved rather badly. I have said that he must apologise to you in person. With this in mind, he requests a meeting with you after lunch."

Rosaleena's heart quailed.

"I accept his apology in advance. He does not need to meet with me. I am sure that he has a – sore head."

"Indeed he has," agreed Sir Uriel, regarding her closely. "We have had a prodigious amount of ice sent up from the ice house. Nevertheless he is bent on seeing you alone. I suggest the library at two o'clock."

Throwing down his napkin, he then left the room.

"It is so good of your Uncle Uriel not to allude to your – unbecoming conduct with Colonel Joyce," observed Lady Rosscullen.

"What need has he to do so," countered Rosaleena crossly, "when you undertook the task yourself?"

She was immediately contrite when she saw tears well up in her mother's eyes.

"I am so sorry, Mama," she said hastily. "I think I have something of a sore head myself."

Lady Rosscullen wiped away her tears.

"I am sure you have, my dear. All the excitement is enough to turn anyone's head. And then – the Colonel's flattery."

"F-flattery?" repeated Rosaleena.

"Oh, I can imagine his sweet words," added Lady Rosscullen bitterly. "He quite swept Lalage away too."

Rosaleena silently toyed with her knife and she did not like to think of him whispering words of 'flattery' to Lalage Fonders.

The morning was spent admiring the many birthday presents that guests had brought last night. Rosaleena tried to interest herself in the silk purses, the writing cases and the ostrich feathers, but her mind was elsewhere.

Between her longing to see the Colonel again and her distaste for the coming interview with Oswald, she felt in a complete spin.

Every so often she glanced up at the ormolu clock on the mantelpiece.

It was twelve o'clock and no doubt the Colonel was at this moment arriving at Lady Fonders' house in Cadogan Street and Lalage would be in the tiled hall to greet him.

Rosaleena tried to console herself with the idea that Lalage might not look too well this morning. Perhaps she had deep dark circles under her eyes from the four or five glasses of wine she had watched her drink at supper.

The pleasure of imagining Lalage off-colour and out of sorts soon paled and Rosaleena knew that her friend would rather resort to her mother's rouge pot than appear at less than her best.

All too soon the hall clock struck two.

With a heavy tread she walked to the library.

Oswald was there and she closed the double doors behind her and waited, regarding her cousin from what she deemed was a safe distance.

She could not forget his rough embraces last night.

Oswald coughed and then brought something from behind his back. It was a very large bouquet, so lavish and beribboned that Rosaleena felt embarrassed.

He held the flowers out to her awkwardly.

"These are for you, cousin."

"Thank you," she said, but she did not take them.

"You wanted to see me?" she prompted, wishing not to prolong the ordeal.

Oswald coughed again.

"I behaved – like an idiot last night. I am so sorry."

Rosaleena was surprised at what she recognised as sincere penitence, although, whether it was due to having upset her or to having incurred the fury of his father, she could not tell.

"I accept your apology," she said in a low voice.

She felt for the door handle behind her, anxious to leave, but Oswald stepped forward.

"I don't want you just to accept my apology," he said. "I want you to – forgive me."

Rosaleena lowered her gaze to the floor.

"Of course I – forgive you, Oswald. That is the Christian thing to do."

Oswald sounded brighter with his next question.

"You will forget the matter then?"

"I will – forget the matter."

Oswald visibly relaxed. He picked up the flowers and held them out again.

"I went to Covent Garden to choose these for you."

"I am very grateful."

"I hope your forgiveness indicates that I may feel free to pay you such little attentions from now on?"

Rosaleena's spirits sank even further. She realised that this was a hint that Oswald – and his father and her mother – wished for the subject of marriage to be pursued again once the dust of last night had settled.

But for her it could never settle. She was hungry to experience again the sensations that had flooded through her when in the embrace of Colonel Joyce.

Oswald could never make her pulse race, her heart soar.

At the same time she knew now that this was not the moment to make her feelings clear.

"Nothing is impossible," she said, hoping that this would satisfy Oswald.

It did.

"Well, that will please Papa," he managed to smile.

To Rosaleena's horror, he now advanced, bouquet held out. Forced at last to take it from him, she quickly buried her face into it to hide her disquiet.

She heard him breathing heavily for a moment and then his hand reached for her free hand.

His damp thin lips then kissed her flesh.

She suppressed an involuntary shudder and forced herself to look up as Oswald raised his head from her hand.

"In the end, cousin," he stated with a slight sneer, "one kiss is much the same as another. It's a lesson you will soon learn."

'Never, never,' Rosaleena intoned silently, but even as she did so she knew that the lesson Oswald alluded to was one that he was determined to teach her himself!

# CHAPTER THREE

That evening a letter was brought in on a tray for Sir Uriel where he sat with Rosaleena and her mother by the drawing room fire.

Sir Uriel opened it and gave a snort.

"It's from that wretch, Colonel Joyce," he said.

Rosaleena's heart skipped a beat as he glanced at her and then read the letter aloud,

*"Dear Sir Uriel,*

*I must thank you for granting me the hospitality of your house. I passed a most enlightening evening. Please convey my greetings to Lady Rosscullen and her daughter.*

*Yours etc,"*

"If there's one thing I detest, its sarcasm!" growled Sir Uriel, before crumpling up the letter and throwing it contemptuously aside.

For the next hour Rosaleena eyed it where it lay just beyond the fender.

When her uncle retired and while her mother dozed, she hurriedly retrieved it and tucked it into her bosom.

Later in bed she studied it avidly by candlelight, as if she might detect some hidden message in his words.

At last she blew out the candle and settled herself to sleep, but not before slipping the letter under her pillow.

For the next few days, Rosaleena waited hopefully for a letter of her own from the Colonel.

In the meantime, Oswald contrived to put himself at Rosaleena's service whenever he could.

He would run to hand her in and out of the carriage, go upstairs for her shawl if she forgot it, stoop to pick up her fan or her glove if she dropped either.

Even Rosaleena had to acknowledge the strength of his persistence, while Lady Rosscullen continued to sing his praises at every opportunity.

"What a helpful young man he has become! What a fine leg he has in a pair of breeches!"

Rosaleena found it expedient never to respond and that way, she could never be contradicted, but her mother began to interpret her silence as tacit approval.

"I am sure my daughter is beginning to think more kindly about Oswald," she ventured hopefully at breakfast.

Sir Uriel pursed his lips.

"And then why should she not? Families and their fortunes often fall apart when the children marry outside."

She could not help but dwell on Sir Uriel's mention of the word 'fortune'.

She knew this alluded to her own money that had not been released into her control. Sir Uriel had explained patiently that the Solicitor in Ireland, Mr. McEvoy, had not yet sent on the relevant papers for her to sign.

Not that she should bother her head with accounts, her uncle had added. He would continue to act for her in that matter, if she should so wish.

'I am not sure I do wish,' Rosaleena had thought, but she had not voiced her lack of certainty aloud.

She looked up now as Lady Rosscullen folded her napkin and rose.

"Rosaleena, I forgot to tell you that we are expected at Lady Fonders' at eleven o'clock."

"Mama! I am not ready. When is the carriage?"

"Half-past-ten, no later,"

Rosaleena curtseyed to her mother and Sir Uriel and then rushed from the room.

'*Lady Fonders, Lady Fonders*,' she sang to herself as she ran up the stairs. At last she might hear some news of the Colonel, for had he not been invited to lunch at Cadogan Square the day after the ball?

She and her mother arrived at Lady Fonders' house.

"Oh, my dears," cried that estimable lady from her sofa as the visitors entered. "How miserable I was to miss the ball. But I heard all about it from Lalage and her new friend, the charming Irishman, Colonel Joyce. He has been to visit here on at least three occasions."

Rosaleena gulped.

"Oh. We have not seen him since – since the ball."

Lady Rosscullen threw a warning glance at her. The Colonel's role in having the ball brought to an abrupt end was not generally known. Sir Uriel had merely said that Rosaleena was indisposed and had retired to her room.

Lady Fonders sniffed.

"Well, I should not say it, but Sir Uriel is not one for parties. It's a wonder he agreed to host one at all."

She patted the cushion beside her.

"Now, Rosaleena dear, do come and sit beside me. I hope you have recovered from all the excitement?"

Rosaleena gave a smile as she sat down.

"Yes, Lady Fonders."

"Well, you are a delicate little thing, as I explained to the Colonel. He could not hear enough about you."

"A-about me, Lady Fonders?"

Rosaleena did not look at her mother, although she sensed her alarm.

"Yes, indeed!" Lady Fonders gave Rosaleena's arm a squeeze. "You naughty girl! Were you casting spells?"

"I should hope not!" came in Lady Rosscullen, her manner indignant. "She hardly knows the man."

Lady Fonders sighed.

"Oh, but what a man! He fought in the Peninsular War, did you know? These Irish. So full of dash and, of course, they have the wildest hearts in the world."

"And the least true natures," Lady Rosscullen set her lips grimly.

Rosaleena raised her eyes to her mother's, puzzled yet again by this seemingly new found vehemence towards her late husband's countrymen.

"I cannot claim to be an expert on their nature," said Lady Fonders thoughtfully. "I should think, though, that a man such as the Colonel would have no end of temptation put in his way. My own daughter is a case in point. Indeed, if I was ten years younger myself – "

"Oh, hush with such talk in front of the girl," cried Lady Rosscullen.

Rosaleena, of course, wanted to hear more, but they were now distracted by the sound of the door opening.

It was Lalage, with a large blue feather bobbing on a band about her forehead and Rosaleena, mindful of her manners, rose to embrace her friend.

"Have you given Rosaleena her gift yet, Mama?" Lalage asked her mother.

"Goodness me, I had totally forgotten!" cried Lady Fonders. "And here it is on the table."

Rosaleena then opened the small pink box with the greatest care. Inside was a velvet band similar to the kind that Lalage was wearing, only with a pink feather attached.

"Oh – how original," smiled Rosaleena doubtfully.

"Do you like it? I chose it for you," Lalage said. "Colonel Joyce was most impressed with mine."

"Was he?"

"Put it on, dear," urged Lady Fonders.

Rosaleena donned the headdress and she soon grew accustomed to the sensation of the feather waving at every turn of her head that she forgot to remove it when she and her mother left.

Lady Fonders, sensing Lady Rosscullen's antipathy to the subject of the Colonel, had not mentioned him again. Neither had Lalage, even though her brown eyes had often rested with a resentful expression on Rosaleena.

The day was so fine that Lady Rosscullen ordered the carriage to wait while she and Rosaleena took a stroll in the square. After a short walk along the outer paths Lady Rosscullen sat down to take some sun.

Rosaleena begged permission to continue her walk.

"Do, my dear," said Lady Rosscullen. "But don't be longer than ten minutes."

Rosaleena then circled the fountain, taking pleasure in the splashing of water into the high stone bowl and then crossed to the pergola on the other side of the square.

Hardly had she advanced a yard along it when she saw someone approach from the opposite direction.

Her heart leapt in her breast as she recognised the figure of Colonel Joyce. He stopped and bowed.

"Miss Rosscullen. What luck to run into you, I was on my way to visit Lady and Miss Fonders."

"Oh?"

Rosaleena, to hide her confusion at the Colonel's admission that he was proposing yet another visit to the Fonders' household, affected an unconcerned air.

"You are a frequent guest, I am told."

The Colonel regarded her closely.

"Only because I understood *you* to be there."

"You thought – I might be there one morning?"

"Precisely!" smiled the Colonel.

She had longed for this moment for some days and now it was here she was filled with a strange trepidation.

The Colonel offered his arm.

"Might we not stroll together, Miss Rosscullen?"

Rosaleena shifted from one foot to the other.

"I-I think not, Colonel Joyce."

The Colonel seemed taken aback.

"Why," he said softly, "you were happy enough to accept refuge in my arms the night of the ball."

Rosaleena raised unhappy eyes to his.

"Yes, but – but that was before – "

The Colonel's brow creased.

"Before what, madam?"

"Before – my mother expressed certain reservations regarding persons of your nationhood," replied Rosaleena.

"Ha!"

The Colonel's expostulation and his darkened brow suggested such anger that Rosaleena shrank away.

She watched as he turned and turned again in the manner of a man seeking some outlet for his rage.

"Thus are the friendliest minds in the world turned by blackguards," she heard him mutter.

"Sir?"

He stared broodingly at her for a moment and, then to her astonishment, he tossed back his head with a laugh.

"What is that on your head, young lady?"

Rosaleena reached up and felt at the feather.

"It was a – a present from Lady Fonders. Lalage chose it."

"To make you look as great a fool as herself, I suppose!" added the Colonel.

With that he then reached forward and plucked the feather from its band.

"Did you ever see a bird," he asked, "with feathers as garishly pink as this?"

"N-no," she admitted. "Not in London, anyway."

As she then took the feather back from the Colonel, their fingers briefly met and she found herself blushing.

She realised that she should leave his company and yet she found herself lingering.

She mentioned that she knew he had fought in the Peninsular War and asked him about Portugal as well as Ireland. He then described the beauty of the two countries so eloquently that she was transfixed.

"And which of the two places do you prefer?" she asked him and he smiled.

"What man ever loves another country as well as his own? The countryside I grew up in is fierce and wild and part of my soul."

"The people of your country, are they wild too?"

"Wild in what way?" asked the Colonel.

"Wild in – in love, for example."

Her companion stopped on the path beside her and regarded her closely although with the hint of a smile.

"This I can tell you, Miss Rosscullen, an Irishman's love is indeed a wilder kind of love than you might find on these genteel shores of England."

Rosaleena trembled in every limb as she heard him.

Her gleaming eyes begged him to take her in his arms, although she dared not voice her desire.

What might have happened then as he gazed back at her was uncertain, as they were interrupted by the voice of Lady Rosscullen.

"Rosaleena!"

Lady Rosscullen now advanced, her eyes sweeping coldly over Rosaleena's companion.

"Colonel!" she acknowledged him curtly.

"Lady Rosscullen." The Colonel bowed.

Lady Rosscullen beckoned to her daughter.

"Come. It's time to go home."

"Yes, Mama. G-goodbye, Colonel Joyce," breathed Rosaleena, her voice weak and nervous.

"Let's hope we meet again soon," said the Colonel.

Lady Rosscullen stiffened.

"Let's hope, Colonel, that we do not."

She held out her hand for Rosaleena to take and hurried her daughter away.

After only a few yards, however, she stopped in her tracks and looked back.

"There really *is* something about him that seems so familiar," she murmured, before urging her daughter on.

*

Sir Uriel was furious when he heard of Rosaleena's encounter in Cadogan Square.

"That scoundrel was lying in wait. He knew that you would appear at Lady Fonders' sooner or later."

Sir Uriel caught her chin tightly between his thumb and forefinger.

"You are to have no further contact with that Irish mountebank. Do you hear me?"

Rosaleena wrenched herself free of his grip.

"Why, Uncle?" she asked boldly.

"Have you forgotten, young lady, that you are now an heiress? The man is clearly after your money."

Rosaleena lifted her head.

"How – clearly?" she demanded.

Sir Uriel threw up his hands.

"Are you such a fool? The fellow has the gall to intrude upon your mother and you at Fortnum's. He wants to know all about your life, a perfect stranger. He has the temerity to accept an invitation without the permission of myself, your Guardian, whom he knows to exist.

"And he is no sooner through my door than he is attempting to seduce you. No doubt he was stalking the premises for days before."

Rosaleena was about to reply in indignation as she suddenly remembered the man she had spotted spying out the house the day before her birthday.

She sank speechless into a chair as a further thought struck her.

The carriage that mysterious gentleman had driven away in was the very same carriage that she had watched Colonel Joyce and Lalage depart in the night of the ball.

It could mean only one thing. Colonel Joyce and the mysterious gentleman were one and the same!

Lady Rosscullen was musing aloud,

"You uncle is surely right, dear. Colonel Joyce did enquire a good deal into your circumstances when we first met and he seemed most interested when you mentioned that you were about to come into your inheritance."

Rosaleena suppressed a moan.

If it was indeed the Colonel who had been watching the house that morning, then it was more than likely that he had followed herself and her mother to Fortnum's. There to sport with them as a spider with a fly, finding out all he needed to know to help him gain his ends.

What Sir Uriel said must be true. The Irishman was no more than a fortune-hunter!

She rose unsteadily to her feet.

"Mama – Uncle Uriel – I don't wish to discuss this anymore, please."

Sir Uriel regarded her for a moment and then gave a nod to her mother.

"She may leave us now," he said.

Rosaleena trailed disconsolately to her room where she tugged the headband from her head.

"What a fool you are, Rosaleena Rosscullen," she cried. "The first handsome stranger who shows an interest in you and you show as much sense as a – as a chicken without a head."

She removed her gown and looked at herself in the mirror in her petticoat and bodice.

This body of hers had betrayed her, yearning so for the Colonel's touch, trembling when he came near.

She traced her lips with her fingers. Was the last remnant of his kiss still there?

Oh my, how he had pierced her heart with his fine words and ingratiating manner.

Fiercely, blinking back tears, she promised herself that she would be coldly circumspect in her dealings with Colonel Joyce, should she ever happen to meet him again.

*

Over the next several days Oswald redoubled his efforts to please and in her disheartened state Rosaleena put up little resistance.

43

Oswald became bolder. He arranged rides out in the carriage as far as Richmond, making sure that the plaid blanket was tucked firmly around his cousin's knees.

Rosaleena could barely put a foot out of the door than he was at her side and, as the weather improved, the open-topped carriage was brought out and made ready.

One afternoon, riding in Hyde Park, Colonel Joyce rode by. Taking in the sight of Oswald at a glance, he did not stop, but tipped his hat politely and rode on.

Oswald could not help but note the obvious distress on Rosaleena's face.

"It's a wonder to see that fellow riding out alone," he remarked coolly. "They say Lalage Fonders is almost always with him these days – she has a large dowry too."

Rosaleena roused herself.

"*Too?*" she repeated shortly.

"Meaning, like yourself. And a dozen other young girls in London who I am sure he would like to become acquainted with."

Rosaleena turned her face away. She felt just as if a jackdaw was pecking at her heart and vowed to think about the Colonel no more.

*

This vow was put to the test only two days later, when she attended a salon at Lady Fonders' house.

Sir Uriel had not wanted to go and had certainly not wanted the ladies to attend as well. But he relented when Oswald promised to accompany his step-aunt and cousin.

Rosaleena knew that the Colonel was very likely to be there and steeled herself to resist his advances.

When he approached to greet her arrival, Rosaleena forced herself to be cold and dismissive, as her mother and Oswald looked on with satisfaction.

The Colonel's features stiffened. With a bow he retired to join a circle at cards.

Rosaleena could not help but glance across to see who else was sitting there with him. Lalage, of course. She raised a hand to wave at her friend, but did not get up.

'The man is shameless,' thought Rosaleena as she took a seat at a table with her mother and Oswald.

She was furious to find her hands trembling as she picked up her cards. She should not allow herself to be so affected by his proximity.

Yet, try as she might, her eye persistently wandered to the table where the Colonel sat.

He looked most distinguished with his raven dark hair glistening in the candlelight, his green eyes glinting as he perused his hand.

When he leaned forward to catch something Lalage said, Rosaleena felt as if a cat was clawing at her breast.

Wracked by such conflicting emotions, desperate to show him that she cared nothing for him, Rosaleena for the first time responded recklessly to Oswald's attentions.

She tapped his arm with her fan, held her head on one side coyly when he spoke to her and lowered her gaze.

Oswald could not believe the effect that he was suddenly having on his cousin and so, at every opportunity, he caught her hand to kiss it, much to Lady Rosscullen's satisfaction and Lady Fonders' amusement.

From the very corner of her eye Rosaleena felt the Colonel watch the proceedings darkly.

'There you are, you feckless Irishman!' she thought with triumph. 'I can be as flirtatious and shallow as you.'

Ten o'clock came and the tables began to break up.

Oswald walked off in the dark to hail the carriage, while Rosaleena went into the hall to wait for her cloak and Lady Rosscullen lingered to say goodbye to Lady Fonders.

Lost in her thoughts, Rosaleena did not see a figure move forward to intercept one of the many maids tripping in and out with cloaks and capes.

The next moment she gave a start as her cloak was draped about her shoulders.

Turning, she saw the Colonel and, before she could say a word, he caught her arm roughly and then drew her protesting along the passage that led to the garden.

Finding a dimly-lit niche, where a marble urn stood on a shelf, he manoeuvred her into an arbour.

She stood panting angrily before him.

"What do you mean by this, sir?" she demanded.

"Ah, Rosaleena, I might well ask what *you* mean by this."

She tossed her head.

"By what exactly?"

"This *froideur*."

"I don't speak French, sir. What does – *froideur* – mean?"

"Coldness, an iciness that would freeze the heart in any breast."

Rosaleena gave a cool smile.

"Not your heart, Colonel, for you have none."

He drew in his breath as if struck. He curled his hand into a fist and brought it hard against the wall.

She cowered beneath him.

"What? You have drunk your uncle's poison?"

"I don't know what you mean, sir!"

The Colonel straightened. He then unclenched his fist and stared at it as if it had formed itself without him.

"I forget myself," he muttered at last.

"I think you do, Colonel," Rosaleena agreed, her eyes never leaving his face. "Did you drag me here to talk about cold hearts and poison?"

He sighed and passed a hand over his forehead.

"No, Rosaleena. I dragged you here, as you put it, for another reason altogether."

"Which is?" Rosaleena asked haughtily.

"Which is to beg you to resist your uncle's plans for yourself and his son."

Rosaleena was aghast.

"What business is it of yours if there is such a plan and if I choose to accept it or not?"

Colonel Joyce leaned his face close to hers.

"I have seen one injustice perpetrated against you," he murmured. "I don't wish to stand by and see another."

Before Rosaleena could respond to this astonishing remark, she heard her mother calling her from the hall.

Her eyes met the Colonel's.

"I – must go," she said quietly.

About to turn, she felt the Colonel's hand fix itself on her wrist as she met his eyes warily.

"Remember my words," he said, "but repeat them to no one. Do you promise?"

Rosaleena hesitated as she realised that she should promise him nothing, but his touch confused her.

Her affected *froideur* – was that the word? – was melting.

Her limbs were beginning to tremble as she felt his breath so close. Her flesh thrilled as he tightened his grip.

Lifting helpless eyes to his, she would promise him anything.

His expression lightened a little and the next instant his lips were on hers.

It was a soft kiss and a long one.

Rosaleena thought she would faint until she felt the Colonel reach an arm about her waist and hold her firm.

And she could never have imagined such pleasure as consumed her frame and burned in her breast.

A moan escaped from her mouth and then she was released.

Shaking, she leaned back against the wall. She had touched the stars and her life would never be the same.

'He must love me, he must love me, to kiss me so,' she thought deliriously.

But when she then gazed up at the Colonel, he had adopted a mocking air.

"I must now bid you adieu," he said, "before I am unmanned entirely by your beauty."

Stung by his levity when she felt so overwhelmed, Rosaleena heard herself lash out bitterly,

"Is it my beauty or is it my *purse* that threatens to unman you?"

The Colonel's expression was unreadable.

"Well, I am in a conundrum about that, for either is a great magnet to a footloose Irishman like myself."

Rosaleena drew herself up to make a suitably tart reply when she caught sight of her mother approaching her behind the Colonel.

He saw her gaze and turned, his eyes locking with those of Lady Rosscullen, who stopped in her tracks.

Rosaleena now wondered at the look of recognition dawning in her mother's eyes before Lady Rosscullen, with a soft cry, sank in a dead faint to the ground.

Without hesitation, Colonel Joyce rushed to catch her up and carry her into the house and, laying her down on a couch, he gestured to the distraught Rosaleena.

"Look to your mother," he ordered, before turning on his heels and vanishing along the passage.

She chaffed her mother's hands between her own.

"Mama, Mama," she sobbed.

At last Lady Rosscullen's eyes fluttered open.

"Is he gone?" she asked, raising her head feebly.

Rosaleena nodded and she struggled to sit up.

"Mama – why did you faint?" asked Rosaleena.

Lady Rosscullen gathered up her shawl from where it had fallen at the side of the couch.

"I am sure I was – quite overcome – in the stifling air," she said carefully. "The fires are banked up far too high for spring."

Rosaleena was not convinced, but her mother made it clear that she would say no more.

They rode back home in silence, Rosaleena stealing glances at her mother's pale and preoccupied face.

Sir Uriel was in the library when they reached the house. Lady Rosscullen dismissed her daughter with a kiss and then knocked at the library door.

She went to her room, where her maid was waiting to help her undress.

It was a long time before Rosaleena slept, her lips burning in the memory of a kiss that should not have been given and her mind tormented by the image of her mother in a dead faint.

# CHAPTER FOUR

Rosaleena's eyes flew open in the dark. What had awakened her? She sat up, drawing the bed quilt around her, and listened.

Footsteps! Footsteps in the street below.

Whoever it was paused outside the house and then mounted the porch steps.

A moment later Rosaleena heard a soft rapping on the front door.

She was overcome with curiosity. Who could be calling at this hour and in such a clandestine manner?

She tiptoed to her bedroom door. There was not a sound in the house.

Carefully Rosaleena descended to the first landing and the head of the stairs.

The visitor rapped again and this time someone in the house responded.

Peering down, Rosaleena could see her uncle come hurriedly out of his study, a candle in his hand.

Sir Uriel crossed the hall and hauled open the door.

A large man in a cloak stood on the threshold and Sir Uriel quickly drew him in.

"I've come as summoned," he said in a gruff voice.

"Ssshh." Sir Uriel put a finger to his lips. "Come into the library. We'll talk in there."

Thoroughly intrigued by now, she did not hesitate. As the two men disappeared into the library, she scuttled as quickly as she dared down the stairs.

In his haste her uncle had left the library door just slightly ajar and she pressed her ear to the crack to listen.

The two men were speaking in low voices and only some of their discussion was audible.

"I am having the devil of a problem with Lady Rosscullen," Rosaleena heard her uncle say. "She wants to inform the authorities that the fellow is in London."

The visitor mumbled and then Sir Uriel snorted.

"I am well aware it's not in our interests to pursue that route! What is in our interests is to keep an eye on the fellow and find out what he is after. For the sake of our own skins."

Through the crack in the door, Rosaleena watched as the visitor eyed Sir Uriel, head on one side. She could not hear what was said, except for the last few words,

" – concerning the girl?"

Sir Uriel grimaced. He turned to the window for a moment and Rosaleena missed the first part of his reply, but, as he turned back, she caught the remainder,

" – designs on Rosaleena. Probably sees it as a way of making reparation in kind."

They now drew nearer to the fireplace, the visitor holding out his hands to the dying embers.

Rosaleena strained to hear what the visitor said next but caught only the unfamiliar name 'Kilvarra'.

This name seemed to disturb her uncle, for Sir Uriel bent and rested his head in his hands.

He repeated 'Kilvarra' in his reply, but Rosaleena could decipher little else.

She stepped quickly back as the two of them shook hands and turned towards the door and then made a run for the stairs and the landing before they came into the hall.

The visitor drew his cloak collar up to his neck.

"Don't you fret, Reece," he said. "I'll run as close as a pup behind our friend."

"You will keep me informed of anything you can find out?"

"I'll keep you informed," promised the visitor and then he stepped out into the night air.

Sir Uriel closed the door and stood leaning against it, staring into space.

Rosaleena drew back, breath still held. She hoped against hope that her uncle did not decide to make his way up to bed, for then she would be lost.

It was with great relief that she saw him finally detach himself from the front door and, candle unsteady in his hand, make his way back to the library.

Rosaleena withdrew to her room, where she curled up beneath the bedclothes with her mind racing.

Why was her mother so keen for the authorities to know that the 'fellow' – surely meaning Colonel Joyce – was in London? And why did Sir Uriel resist this desire of Lady Rosscullen?

Who was the visitor and why was it in his interest as much as Sir Uriel's to keep an eye on the Colonel?

And who or what was 'Kilvarra'?

Her thoughts did not let her rest, but tormented her until the first fingers of dawn crept through the shutters.

Yawning, she slithered further down the bed. She must have dozed off, because the next thing she was aware of was her maid entering with a tray of cocoa and biscuits.

Rosaleena sat up, her hair falling over her face.

The cocoa revived her a little and soon she was up and about, dressing for breakfast.

She frowned as she regarded her white skin and bleary eyes in the mirror and pinched her cheeks to entice a little life into her face.

On her way to breakfast, the library door opened and her uncle unceremoniously called her in.

That he had not gone to bed at all was obvious. His eyelids were swollen, his shirt rumpled and his hair untidy.

Despite the bright day outside, the shutters were all closed up and it was a moment or two before Rosaleena noticed that her mother was sitting at the hearth.

"Sit down." Sir Uriel gestured to Rosaleena to take a seat at the fireplace.

Lady Rosscullen looked up for the first time as her daughter sat down.

"Mama, what is this about?

Lady Rosscullen's lips trembled.

"It's better if you hear it from your uncle."

"Hear – what?"

Sir Uriel came forward, mopping his brow with his handkerchief, then casting nervous glances at the shuttered window as if in fear that some intruder might break in.

"Rosaleena," he began, "you must prepare yourself. We are to – to leave England."

"Leave England?"

Rosaleena looked towards her mother, who raised her eyes and gave a nod of confirmation.

Bewildered, Rosaleena looked back at Sir Uriel.

"Why must we leave, Uncle?"

"You have come of age, Rosaleena, and you have come into your inheritance. It is time that you saw your estate in Ireland. I have written to the housekeeper at Rosscullen House to inform her of our arrival."

Rosaleena, even though she could not admit to her eavesdropping of the night before, suspected a connection between the mysterious visitor and Sir Uriel's decision.

"Why such a sudden departure, Uncle?"

Sir Uriel looked uneasy.

"Your mother and I felt it would be best for you be removed from a certain unwholesome influence."

Rosaleena drew herself up.

"By which you mean Colonel Joyce?" she asked.

"By which I most certainly mean Colonel Joyce," Sir Uriel replied. "He has made his mercenary intentions all too clear."

Rosaleena looked towards her mother. The way that she avoided her gaze convinced Rosaleena that her uncle's explanation for the sudden departure was not the full truth.

She had no time to reflect for a loud commotion at the front door announced the arrival of a visitor.

Lady Rosscullen rose as the library door was flung open to permit the entrance of an agitated Lady Fonders.

"My dears!" she gasped, advancing with one hand clutched dramatically to her throat.

"You will never believe me! It seems that Colonel Joyce has completely disappeared!"

Lady Rosscullen sank back while Sir Uriel paled.

"What do you mean?" he said in a low voice.

Rosaleena leaned forward, heart palpitating, to hear Lady Fonder's reply.

"I sent my coachman to *Buswell's Hotel* early this morning. He was to deliver an invitation for the Colonel and wait for a reply. Well, imagine my consternation when the coachman returned with the news that Colonel Joyce had departed before dawn! He had paid his bill in full, but – and this is quite the mystery – left no forwarding address for those acquaintances like myself and Lalage, who would have expected to see him over the next few days."

Sir Uriel stood as if struck.

"Gone to ground," he groaned unthinkingly.

It was obvious that he almost immediately regretted his remark, as he gave a nervous glance at Lady Rosscullen and resumed the mopping of his brow.

Lady Fonders, meanwhile, gave a tut of surprise.

"Why on earth," she asked imperiously, "should a gentleman such as Colonel Joyce have 'gone to ground'. He did not seem to be a man who had a price on his head."

At this, Lady Rosscullen gave a strangled sob and stopped her mouth with her handkerchief.

"Constance!" asked Lady Fonders. "Are you ill?"

Sir Uriel then flashed a look of annoyance at Lady Rosscullen.

"My stepsister sadly has a touch of indigestion," he explained. "Regarding Colonel Joyce, it has now come to light that he fought under Napoleon, a matter which would be of undoubted interest to the British authorities. I believe he knew that he was found out and decided to flee."

Lady Fonders reeled in shock.

"But you must be mistaken. He told me he fought under Wellington."

Sir Uriel shook his head.

"Dear me, no. My informant could not be wrong."

Rosaleena knew by 'informant' that Sir Uriel must be referring to his visitor of last night.

She too was shocked to discover that Colonel Joyce had fought for the enemy and had lied to her about it.

At the same time she did not believe that this news alone regarding Colonel Joyce would so upset her mother or indeed cause her to faint as she had the night before.

"It's a wonder," Lady Fonders was saying, "that Colonel Joyce took the risk of coming to England at all, the political climate here being such as it is."

"The gall of an Irishman!" said Sir Uriel. "To fight for Napoleon and then come fortune-hunting in the country he betrayed."

"Fortune-hunting?" Lady Fonders echoed.

Sir Uriel nodded.

"I have no doubt he was after Rosaleena's money. Why," he added, with a faint sneer, "I am surprised you did not suspect his interest in your own daughter."

"In Lalage?" Lady Fonders looked uncertain. "She was fond of him, but I thought his interest lay elsewhere, as indeed you are suggesting it did."

Rosaleena sensed Lady Fonders glancing her way as she blushed and lowered her head further.

Sir Uriel gave a grunt.

"If he had no success with my niece, he would no doubt have pursued your daughter. This man is so totally unscrupulous and it is for that reason that we plan to take Rosaleena away."

"Away?" Lady Fonders looked askance. "What, is the whole world deserting me?"

Lady Rosscullen regarded her friend with regret.

"We can take no chances, Fanny. The Colonel may return. We are taking Rosaleena to Ireland, out of reach."

"To Ireland?" scoffed Lady Fonders. "What makes you think that Rosaleena will be beyond the reach of his charms there? The fellow is Irish, for Heaven's sake. It is most likely that he has fled London with the intention of returning to his ancestral home? Take Rosaleena there and you may well throw her right into his path again."

Sir Uriel gave a snort.

"That devil would never go to Ireland. His face is too well known there. No, no. Mark my words. He has returned to the Continent. He would not risk jail."

"Or the gallows," added Lady Rosscullen faintly.

Rosaleena's head jerked up just in time to catch the astonished expression that crossed Lady Fonders' features.

"The gallows?" she repeated.

Lady Fonders was about to continue, but Sir Uriel intervened quickly.

"Lady Fonders, forgive us, you do know how much we value your company, but now we have to arrange for our departure."

Lady Fonders hesitated a second before bowing her head politely.

"I understand, Sir Uriel. You wish to be rid of me. I shall not take it amiss. Constance, be sure to call on me before you finally depart."

"If I can I will," promised Lady Rosscullen. "But – we are leaving within the week."

Lady Fonders raised an eyebrow.

"Well, that is indeed rather sudden," she remarked. "Rosaleena, I will send Lalage to see you before you leave. My poor daughter will be quite bereft."

Rosaleena gave a wan smile as she rose to her feet to kiss Lady Fonders goodbye.

She watched as her mother escorted Lady Fonders into the hall and she saw the two ladies embrace.

Sir Uriel was engaged in peering out between the slats of the shutters, as if checking the street below, though for quite what Rosaleena could not say.

She turned and stared at the heap of cold ash in the grate, pondering miserably on what it was that the Colonel might have done to earn himself a place on the gallows.

*

The ship rose and fell gently in the early evening air as the sea splashed at its sides.

Ahead the Irish coastline approached.

Rosaleena stood at the prow, her eyes fixed on the horizon and the mountain range that rose out of the sea.

She was looking at the country where she was born. The country where Colonel Joyce was born. It was the country where her father had died and the country whose men her mother so reviled.

No wonder she felt confused about its place in her heart.

It was not after all the country where she had grown up. That was in England and it was England that Colonel Joyce had betrayed.

'*He is a liar and a traitor*,' Rosaleena told herself fiercely.

Why then did his kiss still linger on her lips, why did her body ache to feel his arms about her?

'There is something perverse and wicked in me,' she decided sternly.

Something *wild* perhaps! This last thought sent an illicit thrill through her. Did she and the Colonel, then, have something in common?

Leaning on the rail, she brooded on all that had led to this moment.

There was more about the affair of Colonel Joyce than she could fathom, but neither Sir Uriel nor her mother would discuss him with her.

During their last week in London, Sir Uriel had continued to exhibit signs of great anxiety. He barely left the house and kept the shutters in the library closed.

Rosaleena had the distinct impression that he was afraid, although she could not imagine that it was Colonel Joyce who haunted him so.

Whoever or whatever it was, Sir Uriel did not relax until he was on the ship sailing away from England.

Lalage had called to say her farewell. She had been somewhat subdued and at last had blurted out that she had fallen half in love with the Colonel and did not believe for an instant he was the villain everyone now said he was.

Rosaleena, who felt she knew better, did not see the point in disabusing her friend. Besides, she wanted to find out what she could about the Colonel

"Did Colonel Joyce ever – kiss you?" she asked as casually as she could.

"Kiss me?" Lalage had sighed. "If only he had."

Rosaleena tried not to feel too self-satisfied.

"But he did – flatter you?" she pressed.

Lalage plucked at the beads of her necklace.

"He said I had rather nice teeth," she said at last.

"Nice teeth?"

"The truth is," Lalage confessed, "he did not care for me half as much as he cared for you. It's not fair. I used to like Oswald and now *he* is pursuing you as well."

Rosaleena barely registered Lalage's confession of once liking Oswald. She was still thinking of the Colonel.

"You do know that the Colonel is a fortune-hunter, don't you?" she said.

Lalage tossed her head disdainfully.

"If he really is a fortune-hunter, he would surely have pursued *me* rather than you. As I stand to inherit far more money."

Rosaleena had given a start as she realised that this was indeed the case.

She turned now as she heard a voice behind her, shouting against the stiff breeze.

It was Oswald.

He staggered to the rail beside her as the ship gave a sudden pitch.

"I shall never make a sailor," he groaned, his pallor somewhat green.

Rosaleena regarded him with mild concern.

"Should you not stay below if you feel seasick?"

"I would far rather be up here with you."

Rosaleena looked away.

She wondered if, in her intention to banish Colonel Joyce from her mind, she had not perhaps paid her cousin more attention than was wise.

As the ship steadied itself and plunged on, his hand now crept towards hers along the rail.

Rosaleena lifted her hand quickly and pointed at the advancing coastline.

"Does Ireland not look enchanting?"

Oswald was not impressed and clearly piqued that she had removed her hand from his attempted grasp.

"It's nothing like the White Cliffs of Dover. I am most put out at having to come to this place of bogs and barbarians. If you had not encouraged that Irish fellow's attentions, I could be snug in my Club this very minute."

His sudden rancour was wounding and tears sprang to Rosaleena's eyes.

Oswald regarded her with a certain satisfaction.

"Serves you right that the Colonel turned out to be a scoundrel! You had better forget him and start thinking of me. It's with me the future lies. That's what Papa says and he is always right."

Rosaleena shrank back from his certainty. Noting this, Oswald reached under her cloak and pinched her arm hard and then laughed at her squeal of pain.

"I am not such a bad fellow, Rosaleena. You would have a better time with me than you imagine, for I am not inexperienced with women."

"As you have told me before," retorted Rosaleena, rubbing her arm furiously.

The ship's horn sounded, drowning Oswald's reply and Lady Rosscullen and Sir Uriel joined them.

The four figures now stood lost in their individual thoughts as the vessel slid into Dublin harbour.

The *Gorey Hotel* carriage was waiting on the dock.

Rosaleena stared about her as they rattled through the streets, revelling in the sights of this unfamiliar City.

She was exhausted and slept deeply that night.

*

On the following morning a hired coach arrived to take them to the hinterland.

Rain was falling, so softly it was almost like mist. Rosaleena barely felt the drops on her face as she turned it up to the silver grey sky before climbing into the vehicle.

The coach left the City travelling West. It rolled along a narrow road, the landscape on each side flat and lush, the grass dazzlingly green.

That night, they stopped at a country inn and ate a supper of rich Irish stew.

Oswald complained bitterly the next morning that his stomach had suffered and he had hardly slept because his mattress was full of lumps.

Rosaleena laughed as she had slept like a baby.

That day progress was slower. The carriage turned South-West and the road was more like a track.

The clouds of yesterday had cleared and a warm sun as yellow as buttermilk hovered over the rising hills.

It was very nearly dusk when at last they rolled in through the open gates of the Rosscullen estate.

Rosaleena peered eagerly about her.

"Is this really all mine?" she asked.

"All yours," replied her mother in a faltering voice.

"It's all yours," echoed Sir Uriel with a meaningful look at Oswald.

"Well, I don't think much of it," sniffed Oswald. "It's nothing but weeds and soggy grass."

Rosaleena ignored him.

From what she could see she thought the estate was beautiful. There was a wild uncultivated look about it, so different to the pruned and clipped acres that surrounded English country houses.

Fuschia dripped from the hedgerows and blood red rhododendrons, like big hearts, were everywhere.

Sheep cropped the grasses and Rosaleena thought with sudden pride that these flocks were hers as well.

She had been a baby when she left this place. She could not possibly remember the landscape or the house.

And yet, as the house veered into her view, she was suffused with an emotion that made her heart pound.

It had a grey stone façade with long elegant sash windows. At either end, the walls curved out to create a bow effect and each bow boasted a set of tall windows.

There was a well-manicured lawn that dipped on the right towards an area of rock and ravine and on the left ran to a border of oak trees, old, gnarled and majestic.

Rosaleena's heart seemed to sing in her breast.

'*I am coming home*,' she thought with exhilaration. 'I am really coming home.'

It was at that very moment that her mother began to weep and no one moved to comfort her.

Sir Uriel, Oswald and Rosaleena herself, sat frozen. It was as if this manifestation of distress was an inevitable accompaniment to the rattle of the carriage over stone and the loud cawing of rooks in the trees.

Lady Rosscullen's weeping grew in volume as the carriage drew up before the house, until her sobs rang out inconsolably in the darkening air.

It was only then that Rosaleena reached out and gently put a hand on her mother's knee.

"Mama," she urged. "Dry your eyes, we are here."

She turned as the front door of Rosscullen House flew open, releasing a flood of golden light from within.

A small figure came out, holding a lantern aloft and a voice called out to the arrivals.

"Welcome, welcome. The house is ready for you."

A boy raced up to open the carriage door.

He extended his hand and Rosaleena stepped out, before her mother and before her uncle and cousin, as if to establish that this was her very Kingdom, the place of her heart, the long lost home of her hungry soul.

# CHAPTER FIVE

The woman who had called out the welcome was the housekeeper, Mrs. Lynch. She had been at Rosscullen House since the time of Rosaleena's grandfather.

Rosaleena had always imagined that she must then be very ancient, yet this tiny lady, despite her halo of white hair, seemed to have the energy of someone half her age.

Mrs. Lynch darted forward as Lady Rosscullen was helped from the carriage.

"Your Ladyship," she cried out with emotion. "You have returned! I thought I'd never see the day."

Rosaleena watched as her mother and Mrs. Lynch embraced. Sir Uriel looked on from the carriage door.

At last the two women drew apart and Mrs. Lynch turned her bright bird-like eyes upon Rosaleena.

"And this will be Rosaleena! Sure to Heaven you have the look of your poor father on you!"

Sir Uriel descended heavily from the carriage.

"More of her mother, I think," he muttered tightly.

Mrs. Lynch regarded him with an expression that Rosaleena, with some degree of surprise and not a little pleasure, recognised as disdain.

"Well, sir. How are you?" she asked him politely.

Sir Uriel ignored the question. He bent down and looked intently into the little woman's face.

"I hope my instructions have been carried out?"

"To the letter," she replied, unflinching in his gaze.

"Good woman," grunted Sir Uriel, straightening up.

Rosaleena now wondered what these 'instructions' might be as the party moved towards the house.

Once inside the graciously wide hall of Rosscullen House, however, she forgot her thoughts of a moment ago.

Happily she breathed in the scent of hyacinths and wax polish, imagining that she remembered it.

She was taken upstairs by a plump nervous girl who told Rosaleena that she had been hired only the day before.

"And are you settling in, Mary?" asked Rosaleena, trying to put the poor girl at her ease.

"I am, miss," returned the girl gratefully. "I know half the workers here. Sure, weren't the whole crowd of us hired at the same time!"

Rosaleena looked at her in surprise.

"You are all new here then?"

Mary nodded.

"Only Mrs. Lynch has been here since the days of Lord Rosscullen. All the others were then dismissed when the house was shut up after – "

She broke off, hand at her mouth.

"After my father's death?" Rosaleena finished for Mary calmly.

The girl nodded, eyes guilty.

"Yes, but – we were told not to mention that or we would be sacked in an instant. My tongue should be sliced off, so it should."

"Then I will not say a word to anyone," Rosaleena reassured her.

The two set off again, up a flight of stairs and along a wide corridor.

Rosaleena was thoughtful as she followed Mary.

So that was what Sir Uriel's 'instructions' had been – Mrs. Lynch was to employ new servants and order them never to mention the death of young Lord Rosscullen.

Mary stopped and flung open a door.

"Your room, miss."

It was a lovely room. The walls were all hung in a Chinese silk that had faded to a pale gold. A large enamel tub was drawn up before a marble fireplace in the hearth of which a log fire merrily crackled.

A *chaise longue* in dove-blue material stood near the long windows. The vista beyond was of lawn scattered with buttercups, leading to the rocky and romantic ravine.

Half an hour later, Rosaleena was luxuriating in an enamel bathtub, her face turned to the glow of the fire and, after all the emotional turbulence of the last week, she was almost at perfect peace.

The reason that it was not complete peace was the memory of the Colonel.

It seemed more difficult than ever to cast him from her mind, surrounded as she was by people who had the same lilt in their voices.

She gazed dreamily down at her body, idly noting its pearly sheen beneath the water.

For a brief second she imagined the Colonel there, gazing down at her in admiration.

She flushed as she realised where her thoughts had led her. She slid down under the water as if to wash away the image of the Colonel entirely.

Then she rose and reached blindly for the towel on the nearby rack.

"I have it."

The voice was unfamiliar and Rosaleena shook her wet hair out of her eyes to see who it belonged to.

A tall young woman stood there, a light smile on her red lips, the towel lying across her arm.

"I am your personal maid," the young woman said introducing herself. "I am Bridie."

The smile widened as she held out the towel.

Rosaleena did not move. As there was something about her – Bridie – that mesmerised her. Something in her fiery intelligent features seemed almost familiar.

"You will be catching your death of cold standing there without a stick on you!" Bridie warned.

Rosaleena was startled. Bridie might be a maid, but she was not in the least way deferential. She had not once addressed Rosaleena as 'miss'.

Intrigued, she at last stepped out of the bath.

Bridie then began to dry her, rather too briskly for Rosaleena's liking.

"Were you hired yesterday as well?" she asked the maid over her shoulder.

"I was," Bridie replied. "But I could not sleep here last night as the others did."

"You will be sleeping here from now on?"

"I will indeed," replied Bridie shortly. "There, you are dry. What will I get you now?"

Rosaleena was surprised that Bridie did not know.

She indicated the clean clothes laid out on the bed by Mary, who had obviously been standing in for Bridie.

Rosaleena wondered if this was the first time Bridie had worked in this capacity, but she hesitated to interrogate the young woman.

"Have you been a maid before?" she asked at last.

"No. But I am a quick learner."

She turned to meet Bridie's steady gaze. Again, the green eyes and dark lashes unsettled her.

"What made you take on this position if you were not trained for it?"

"There isn't a great deal of work in this area," said Bridie. "Mrs. Lynch knew I was not experienced, but she knows that I am a willing worker. Does that satisfy you?"

Rosaleena now found herself almost apologetic, so haughty was Bridie's demeanour.

"I-I would not query any of Mrs. Lynch's choices."

"We'll get on," said Bridie and returned to her task.

Having buttoned up Rosaleena's dress, she stepped back to admire her handiwork.

"That's a grand dress," she said, almost resentfully. "And here's a fine shawl to add the finishing touch."

Rosaleena's brow creased. Had she detected a hint of mockery in Bridie's tone?

"We will get on better, Bridie," she said softly, "if you remember that we are as yet unused to each other."

She meant to warn Bridie not to be overfamiliar so early in their relationship. To her surprise, Bridie gave a toss of her head, a strange laugh and replied,

"We will get on well if you remember that you are now in Ireland, but I admire you for your warning."

Rosaleena really could not make Bridie out. If she did not know better she could have taken the young woman to be someone of aristocratic blood.

The supper gong sounded.

Bridie opened the door for Rosaleena and followed her out into the passage.

Mary was hovering there and Bridie ordered her to have the bath in Rosaleena's room emptied.

Mary curtseyed, her eyes wide at seeing Rosaleena in her evening finery.

Rosaleena had barely taken three paces along the passage when a portrait on the wall caught her attention.

She stopped enquiringly before it.

"Do you know who that is?" asked Bridie.

Rosaleena shook her head.

"No. But I feel as if I should."

"Indeed you should. For it's your father."

Rosaleena caught her breath because she had only ever seen a miniature of her father.

She went closer and put a hand up to the face.

"He was – so handsome," she breathed.

"More so in the flesh," murmured Bridie.

Rosaleena turned wonderingly.

"You – knew him?"

She thought that it was not impossible, for Bridie seemed older than herself.

Bridie appeared to choose her words with care as she replied,

"Your father used to come to Kilvarra Castle to visit his close friend, the Irish Earl of Kilvarra. I was only four years old, but I do remember Lord Rosscullen well. I was the gatekeeper's daughter and your father was always very good to me."

Rosaleena, listening intently for information about her father, was nevertheless struck by the name 'Kilvarra' and she was certain she had heard it somewhere before.

The gong sounded again. So Rosaleena dismissed Bridie and then made her way down to the dining room.

A long oak table ran nearly the entire length of the room. Silver gleamed in the light of flickering candles. At one end of the room flames leapt high in a huge hearth.

She settled herself in her seat, after acknowledging her mother and Oswald, as well as Sir Uriel, who sat at the head of the table farthest from the fireplace.

All through supper her mind returned to what she had learned regarding her father and the Earl of Kilvarra.

As dessert was served to them, Sir Uriel and Lady Rosscullen fell to discussing the neighbourhood.

"I hope we plan to throw a ball or large supper party," observed Oswald. "I shall just die of boredom here without lively company."

Sir Uriel and Lady Rosscullen exchanged a glance.

"I think that we should not mix too greatly with our neighbours," he said. "After all, we are English gentlemen and have little in common with them."

Rosaleena was convinced that this reluctance of Sir Uriel and her mother to invite anyone local to Rosscullen House was due to fear, fear that some local visitor would inadvertently bring up the subject of her father's death.

'Really,' she thought to herself, 'it is becoming ever more irritating to be *so* protected.'

Looking down the long table at Sir Uriel, she now decided to speak.

"There is one person we should consider inviting, surely?" she ventured brightly.

Oswald looked hopeful, while Sir Uriel paused and considered Rosaleena over his spoonful of tart.

"Have you heard about an Englishman in residence nearby?" he asked blithely. "I would be surprised. The English landlords don't usually visit their Irish estates until the summer, if at all."

"Oh, this person is not English," replied Rosaleena. "He was a close friend of my Papa's and so I should like to meet him."

"Who are you speaking of, my dear?" asked Lady Rosscullen, her spoon in mid-air, her voice tremulous.

"The Earl of Kilvarra," said Rosaleena quickly.

She could not have anticipated the response.

Her mother dropped her spoon with a cry, while Sir Uriel appeared to choke and Oswald jumped up to clap him on his back.

"I don't where you heard of the Earl," spluttered Sir Uriel, shrugging off his son and now pointing his spoon at Rosaleena, "but I can tell you that he no longer lives at Kilvarra nor in Ireland. And you must never, never suggest inviting him here or mention his name again. Unless you really wish to destroy your mother's health!"

Rosaleena was shaken.

One quick look at her mother's pale and trembling features convinced her that her uncle was in earnest. She bent her head and finished her dessert in silence.

Rosaleena retired to her room early. Brushing her own hair, she watched in the mirror as Bridie turned down her bed and shook out her nightgown.

"Bridie," she asked after a moment, "when was it that you last saw the Earl of Kilvarra?"

Bridie laid her nightgown on the bed carefully.

"The Earl left Kilvarra Castle for good when I was five years old," she said without looking round.

Rosaleena sighed, tapping the back of her hairbrush against her teeth.

"Why on earth does my mother not want his name mentioned?" she wondered aloud.

Bridie turned and looked at her in the mirror.

"I know why," she muttered in a low voice.

Rosaleena met her maid's eyes questioningly.

71

Bridie moved close and laid a hand on Rosaleena's shoulder. She regarded her Mistress gravely.

"The reason is this," she said softly. "It was the Earl of Kilvarra who found your father's dead body!"

*

Rosaleena stood in the long grass, head on one side, listening to the tap of a woodpecker in an old oak.

Yellow butterflies danced in the air before her and fuschias dripped like red tears in the hedgerows.

She had been at Rosscullen for three days now and was fast falling prey to its charms.

Whenever the weather permitted – and though there was much rain, it never fell for too long – she wandered out alone to explore her domain.

Oswald rarely offered to accompany her. He was growing more sullen by the day. Torn from his card games and his London haunts, he was at a loss.

"It's all your fault that we are here," he complained more than once to Rosaleena.

"That is most foolish," she would reply. "Sooner or later I would have to come to take control of Rosscullen."

"Well, I wish it had been later," sniffed Oswald. "And I wish it had been with my ring on your finger, then Papa could have done most of the work and we could have gone home to London. As it is, we are condemned to be here the whole summer, if not longer."

Rosaleena did not reply. Her money had still not been released and she was beginning to suspect the hand of her uncle in this.

It was he, after all, who was in contact with Mr. McEvoy, the lawyer. Until she had full control over her fortune, she could not proceed with her plans for the estate, plans that were evolving in her mind all the time.

She had decided that if Mr. McEvoy did not appear by the end of the week with the necessary papers for her to sign to release her funds, then she would go to him.

She was convinced that her uncle was stalling the legal process in the hope that she would accept Oswald's proposal and he would then continue to run Rosscullen as his son would be the lawful owner.

'Then he will wait a very long time,' she mused. 'It would take more than solitude for me to take Oswald as my husband.'

Rosaleena shook herself free and looked around.

The yellow butterflies were now dancing about her head, so that she felt she could catch handfuls of them.

Although she enjoyed all her wanderings, she could never quite dispel from her mind the idea of the Earl of Kilvarra coming across the body of her father.

She had wanted to find out more from Bridie, but the maid had clammed up after that one revelation, saying that Rosaleena should go to her mother for details.

But that, of course, was something that Rosaleena did not feel free to do. It was obvious that her mother could not bear to be reminded in any way of the loss of her husband, although it did seem hard on the Earl, who had merely been unlucky enough to find the body.

The mere idea that her father's body was 'found' disturbed Rosaleena. It suggested that he had not died surrounded by his family and friends, but had been stricken down in some way far from Rosscullen House.

Perhaps in the grounds she was now walking on.

If so, she only hoped that it was on a day as balmy as this. So that when the Earl of Kilvarra found him, he would have been at peace.

Rosaleena wondered if the death of his friend was the reason why the Earl had left his home and his country.

She could find no face for the Earl and in her daydreaming he had gradually assumed the features of the one Irishman she knew at all intimately – Colonel Joyce.

The two men had become inextricably fused in her imagination, although one she had never met and the other she would never set eyes on again.

Rosaleena sighed.

The gentle air and sweet scents made her restless as her surroundings were undeniably romantic and here she was without romance.

She struggled every day to remind herself that the Colonel was a villain, but could not forget how she had nestled against his breast after fleeing from Oswald.

The sun on her lips now could not burn them more fiercely than had his eager kiss.

She walked on, the butterflies parting in front of her and then meeting again in a yellow cloud behind her.

An unearthly stillness reigned around her and her troubled mind seemed soothed.

A rustle of grass alerted Rosaleena to the fact that someone was nearby.

She turned and spied Bridie coming towards her with a basket over her arm.

"I have been in the orchard and have a wealth of apple blossom here," Bridie explained. "Look."

The basket was indeed full of blossom, frothing up like pink foam.

Yet Rosaleena was overcome with the impression that Bridie had deliberately set out to waylay her, although why she could not think.

Whatever Bridie's motives might be, she welcomed the company and invited her to walk with her.

They fell in side by side and Rosaleena was now even more convinced of her suspicions as it was apparent that Bridie was discreetly directing their steps.

Neither of them spoke, as if reluctant to break the all-enveloping silence of the day.

Soon they had entered the area of the rocky ravine.

Rosaleena found herself scrambling up and down slopes, clambering over rocks, leaping from promontory to promontory in Bridie's wake.

She refused to protest, even when her dress caught and ripped. She would not allow Bridie the satisfaction of thinking that her Mistress was too soft for a country life!

She heard the waterfall before she saw it, a sound rending the air and shattering the peace. It was some time before she actually stumbled into a clearing and saw it.

It fell thirty feet or so from a barren bluff, a great gushing wall of sound, drumming down into a horseshoe-shaped pool at its base.

She gasped and Bridie threw her a triumphant look. This was obviously why she had led Rosaleena on.

"Isn't it a grand sight altogether? I have heard that in the Earl's day that there would be regular picnics here and swimming."

"Swimming?"

Rosaleena stared dubiously at the pool. It was true that away from the waterfall, the surface was calm, but, she shuddered to herself, it must be cold.

She joined Bridie at the side of the pool, where the two sat on a flat rock.

Rosaleena looked about her curiously. On the other side there was a small Chapel with the roof half gone.

Bridie followed Rosaleena's gaze.

"That was once the private Chapel of one of your Rosscullen ancestors. It has long fallen into disuse."

Beyond the Chapel the landscape opened to reveal on the horizon the outline of a mountain range,

"What mountains are those?" Rosaleena pointed.

"The Slieve Bloom," replied Bridie softly.

"And where is – Kilvarra Castle? Is it near here?"

Bridie gestured with her head towards the horizon.

"In the middle of that mountain country," she said. "A place of mist and shifting sunlight and glinting rock."

Her voice was full of such longing that Rosaleena was surprised.

After a moment she ventured to say that she would like to visit Kilvarra Castle and this time Bridie threw her an almost vehement look.

"Why would you? It's a ruin now. The rooks build their nests in the tower and rain comes through the roof."

"Why is it a ruin?" asked Rosaleena.

She shrank back as Bridie leapt angrily to her feet.

"Because of you!"

"M-me?" Rosaleena was astounded.

"You and your kind!" cried Bridie. "The English."

Rosaleena stared.

"I don't understand," she said at last. "And anyway – I am not all English. My father was Irish, remember."

Bridie appeared to check herself.

"Indeed he was and a good man too," she said.

She observed Rosaleena with rather a troubled air and then suddenly made a decision.

"Come on into the pool," she cried and then began to peel off her boots and stockings.

Rosaleena drew back.

"Oh, I couldn't – it must be freezing."

"You will get used to it," Bridie laughed, slipping out of her skirt.

The next minute she leapt into the water, wearing just her chemise and bloomers.

Rosaleena rose and looked first about her and then back at the pool. Bridie was splashing about like a fish, seemingly unconcerned at the cold.

Rosaleena's hand strayed hesitantly to the buttons of her blouse.

"Come on in, London girl," Bridie beckoned. "It'll clear your head for weeks to come."

So challenging was Bridie's voice that Rosaleena made a decision. Quickly she took off her blouse and skirt and next her shoes and stockings.

Then, hardly daring to think, she threw herself into the glimmering water.

"Oh, oh, oh!"

She almost seized up with the cold. Striking out to warm herself, however, she soon found herself growing accustomed to the chill.

"Did you ever do anything better than this in your whole life?" called out Bridie.

"Never!" giggled Rosaleena.

It was true. She had never felt so carefree or so unburdened. London was all so very far away.

The coldness of her Uncle Uriel, the weakness of her mother, Oswald's behaviour, all vanished. The death of her father, so shrouded in mysteries, ceased to haunt her.

She felt weightless and that invoked a memory. A memory of a time when she had been just as happy if not as free – when her body had felt as light and alive.

Dancing with the Colonel!

Yet even that dance could not compare with this, because its result had led to so much heartache.

If she had not danced with him, she would not have felt herself to be in love. If she had not loved, she could not have felt herself to be betrayed.

Here, in this strange pool, she felt invigorated and now she felt washed clean of the old credulous Rosaleena.

Her heart was her own again. She would cease to yearn for a man who had lied to her, stoked her emotions and disappeared, leaving behind only his sullied reputation.

"I am free, I am free," she sang aloud, turning onto her back and staring up at the azure sky.

"What is it you're saying?" Bridie swam close.

"Nothing. I just am so happy to be alive."

Bridie laughed loudly and, ducking under the water, veered off like a seal.

Rosaleena, moving her arms enough to keep herself afloat, closed her eyes against the dazzle of the sun.

She wondered lazily what time it was. She would like to stay here forever.

'Perhaps I will have a little hut built here for my use,' she thought. 'I could come here with my books and easel and stay all day long.'

She hardly liked to add that here she could dream all day long too.

Rosaleena did not know what it was that made her open her eyes. Her ears were full of the gush of tumbling water so she could not hear any other sound.

Whatever it was, she suddenly sensed that she was under observation and not by Bridie.

She shielded her eyes and looked up.

There, high on the bluff above her, stood the figure of a man. Silhouetted against the sun, she could only see that he was tall, his shoulders broad and he wore a cape.

She cried out at the sight of the intruder and Bridie turned to look.

To Rosaleena's surprise, she showed no alarm, but merely raised her hand in greeting.

The man waved back, then turned and disappeared.

Without a word of explanation, Bridie swam to the edge of the pool and Rosaleena followed.

She climbed out of the pool just as the sun dipped behind a cloud. In sudden shadow, no longer moving, she all at once felt very cold.

Teeth chattering, she watched as Bridie carelessly threw her dress on over her wet under-garments.

"W-who was that man?" she asked.

"A friend," replied Bridie casually.

She glanced at Rosaleena and laughed.

"Cold, are you? Ah, sure, you've no flesh on your bones at all!"

"Now, now," suddenly came a disembodied voice from nowhere. "Remember she has had no cause to grow hardy like yourself."

With that a man stepped from amid the trees and Rosaleena gasped in shock.

There before her stood Colonel Joyce!

# CHAPTER SIX

He seemed taller, darker, wilder.

He had abandoned his martial look altogether.

Now he seemed more like a poet, a plumed hat set at an angle on his head, a jet-black lock of hair falling over his forehead, his eyes green as the moss around the pool.

Rosaleena was struck dumb.

"Y-you!" she finally blurted out.

Colonel Joyce swept off his hat and bowed to her with a somewhat sardonic smile.

"At your eternal service, Miss Rosscullen."

Dazedly Rosaleena shook her head.

"But – but Uncle Uriel said that you would never dare come to Ireland!"

Colonel Joyce looked amused.

"And you take Sir Uriel Reece to be an expert on my character, do you?"

"N-no," stammered Rosaleena. She pushed back her wet hair from her face, regarding him all the while.

"Only, it's little wonder people thought – strange things about you – when you disappeared without a word."

She could not find it in herself to accuse him of being a traitor and a liar. It was all she could do to stop her limbs from trembling, although whether this was because he was there in the flesh or simply because she was cold she could not tell.

The Colonel looked solemn.

"The truth is, I felt a sudden nostalgia for my own country. And how glad I am to discover that its beauty is even more appealing than I remembered."

With a shock Rosaleena realised that he was now perusing her with undisguised admiration.

Conscious that she was soaking wet and her muslin bloomers and chemise were clinging tightly to her body, she blushed and crossed her arms across her breast.

Immediately he apologised for his lack of manners in talking to her when she was so obviously cold.

"Take this," he offered, removing his warm cloak and holding it open for her.

She hesitated, at which the Colonel stepped forward and wrapped the cloak around her. She could detect the scent of wild heather in the material and wondered with a shock if he had been sleeping out under the stars.

He took a leather flask from his pocket, held it to her lips and urged her to take a sip. Obediently she opened her lips and the warm liquid ran through her like fire, reviving her spirit and curiosity.

All this while she had forgotten about Bridie.

Now she could see her maid lingering at a distance, a blade of grass between her lips.

"W-was Bridie instructed to lure me – here to the waterfall?" she asked the Colonel bluntly.

He gave a look of mock apology.

"She was. I was informed you were at Rosscullen and felt a great urge to see you. Since I could not exactly leave my calling card at the house, I could think of no other way but that *you* be led to *me*."

Trying to ignore the way her heart had leapt at the Colonel's admission that he had felt 'a great urge' to see her, Rosaleena drew up her chin.

"Why did Bridie not tell me what she intended in the first place?" she demanded.

"Because then, my dear lady, you would not have come. But here's to our happy encounter!"

With this, he raised the leather flask to his lips, his green eyes fixed on Rosaleena as he drank.

Rosaleena, finally recovering her composure, held his gaze. She told herself that she must not succumb to his charm again after all that she had lately learned about him.

"You are right to say that I would not have come, Colonel," she said coldly. "As, although you may have felt an urge to see me, I felt no such urge to see you, a man who has proved to be a villain and a traitor!"

This last jibe stung.

With a curse Colonel Joyce took the flask from his lips and flung it into the pool and, when he turned back to Rosaleena, his brow was black with anger.

"What do you mean by calling me a traitor?"

Rosaleena felt a little bit less sure of herself now.

"I have heard that people are out for your blood as you enlisted under Napoleon in order to fight the British."

Bridie let out a cry of rage, but the Colonel silenced her with a gesture.

He strode a few feet away and stood staring at the pool, his fists clenched at his side.

She wondered if she should choose this moment to slip away and raise the alarm, but when she looked round for the path, she saw Bridie watching her darkly.

Her eyes flicked back to the figure of the Colonel.

He was breathing hard and deeply and, as her gaze rested with a reluctant admiration on his strong back and wide shoulders, he drew himself up and turned.

"I intend to set my military record straight, Miss Rosscullen," he said, "but before I do that I must extract a promise from you that you will keep my presence here in Ireland a secret. For," he added gravely, "one thing in this is true – there are people out for my blood. Though not for the reasons you have been told."

"What are the reasons, then?" Rosaleena asked him, with a greater courage than she felt.

"He cannot tell you now," called Bridie quickly, a certain impatience in her tone. "Although, God willing, the time will surely come."

The Colonel had not taken his eyes from Rosaleena.

"Do you swear," he demanded fiercely of her, "not to reveal that I am in the country?"

"Why should I swear it?" she asked boldly.

"Because," he replied, "you owe it to your father."

Rosaleena's eyes widened.

"You – you speak as if you knew him!"

"I did know him well and esteemed him greatly and I will carry out what I believe would be his wishes."

Rosaleena closed her eyes for a moment.

This suggested that the Colonel had known who she was all along – just as Sir Uriel had implied.

"Why did you not reveal that you knew my father when we met in London and I told you that – I was from Rosscullen?" she whispered.

The Colonel raised his hand wearily.

"Forgive me, but you are venturing onto a subject that I do not have the heart to discuss. In time you will know all."

Rosaleena choked back a cry of frustration.

"Why is it," she now brooded, "that no one seems to want to discuss my father with me?"

The Colonel, with a gesture of impatience, turned and stared at the blue-black line of the mountains.

"Come, Rosaleena," he said with his back to her. "There's little time to lose. Will you promise not to betray me to my enemies or must I go and leave you convinced I betrayed King and country for the Emperor of France?"

Rosaleena faltered at the sound of her name on his lips. Although he had spoken to her firmly, there had been an unexpected hint of tenderness in his voice.

This more than anything resurrected that moment of supreme happiness when she had danced with him and he had kissed her with such passion.

The memory of swooning in his arms threatened to overcome her so entirely that she felt for the support of a tree or a rock not to show her sudden trembling.

"Promise," the Colonel urged again, turning back to her with a look of anguish on his face.

"I p-promise," she replied in a whisper.

The Colonel held out his hand for her to take. She did so, repressing a shudder as their fingers met.

He directed her to a low rock so scooped out as to resemble a seat and set her down.

Bridie watched them, arms folded over her breast.

Colonel Joyce began by telling Rosaleena that in 1798 misfortune befell his family in Ireland and he was then forced to flee.

"1798," repeated Rosaleena, in a way that indicated that she knew it to be the year of the Irish rebellion.

He quickly assured her that he was not forced to flee for political reasons. Nevertheless, he found himself in France along with many other Irish political *émigrés*.

Like them he was much attracted to the character and ideology of the young Napoleon Bonaparte.

"He spoke of liberty and fraternity," he said. "I was young, seventeen years of age, and impressionable. Along with many Irishmen, I then enlisted in the French army."

It did not take long for him to become disillusioned. When Napoleon made himself the Emperor of France in 1804, he left the country.

He spent some years travelling, visiting Egypt and the Orient, always feeling rootless and without purpose.

Then in 1808 word came that the English had sent a force to Iberia to resist Napoleon's invasion.

"So I made my way to Portugal," he told her, "and enlisted under Wellington."

"So you fought *for* the French and then *against* them?" said Rosaleena with a degree of scorn.

The Colonel regarded her through hooded eyes.

"I fought for a man when I believed him to be a liberator and against him when I discovered him to be a tyrant. But," he concluded, "I think you will agree that the one offence that neither you nor Sir Uriel can accuse me of is ever taking up arms against England."

"And much good your fidelity did you," cried out Bridie before Rosaleena could speak. "Your family shamed – your reputation ruined – your home destroyed. I hope you are not depending on British justice to clear you!"

Rosaleena stared, mouth half open, as the Colonel strode over to Bridie and took her by the shoulders.

"When did I last depend on anyone but myself?" he asked her gravely.

Bridie wrenched her face away from his.

"No time that I remember," she conceded sullenly.

He held Bridie firmly for just a moment longer and then, to Rosaleena's astonishment, leaned down and kissed her lightly on the forehead.

"I think it's time to take your Mistress home," he said with a smile.

Jealously, Rosaleena wondered that he should show such intimacy to a servant.

Bridie's harsh words on the shame of the Colonel's family and the ruin of his reputation were lost on her.

She had heard the Colonel out and believed that he spoke the truth and, now that she could no longer dismiss him as a common traitor, her defences against his charm were demolished.

She had no idea what friendship was now possible between them. If she could not tell Sir Uriel or her mother that she had seen him, she could not tell them that he was innocent of the crimes he was charged with.

If they could not be persuaded of his innocence, she would certainly never be allowed to meet him normally.

"Will I – see you again?" she asked him anxiously.

Looking her way, he gave a nod.

"There is no doubt of that, madam."

"But – how will we meet?" brooded Rosaleena.

"I will find a way, never fear."

The Colonel's gaze rested on her, travelled down her face to her lips and lingered there.

She marvelled as she thought that she detected an expression of hunger enter his eyes.

Rosaleena found herself willing him to come to her, kiss *her* forehead and stare deep into her eyes.

Her body yearned for his touch, her flesh seemed to call to his. She half closed her eyes, as if in anticipation, and her lips opened as if to receive his.

'Come close, come close,' she urged silently.

She heard leaves rustle and footsteps on the stones.

'*He is coming to me*,' she thought happily.

But when she opened her eyes, he had gone.

She blinked back sudden tears, aware that Bridie was watching her with undisguised curiosity.

"It – must be late," she said as airily as she could.

"Come on then," said Bridie gruffly.

She turned on her heels to stride back the way they had come. Rosaleena hurried to fall into step beside her.

Feeling somewhat burdened, she realised with a jolt of pleasure that she still had the Colonel's cloak on her.

She threw a glance at Bridie and then stopped short to see the maid's face streaked with tears.

"What's the matter, Bridie?" she asked curiously.

Bridie wiped her cheek with the back of her hand.

"Nothing," she said fiercely, but her step quickened so that Rosaleena found herself dropping behind.

A cloud black as a crow's wing slid over the sun and Rosaleena gave a shiver. She was glad on more than one count for the cloak, although it weighed heavy on her.

She thought she felt a drop of rain and hastened her step, almost treading on Bridie's heels.

She noted with a certain amount of gall that Bridie had trim ankles and a slender figure. Her dark silky hair flew out about her as she half-walked and half-ran ahead.

Any man would surely find her attractive, thought Rosaleena grudgingly.

She reflected on the way the Colonel had kissed Bridie's forehead and a new and tormenting thought arose in Rosaleena's mind.

Was Bridie in love – with Colonel Joyce?  And – more terrible still to consider – did he love her in return?

*

On her return, Rosaleena hid the Colonel's cloak at the back of the wardrobe in her room

She was so monosyllabic at dinner that her mother asked her if she was ill and, as soon as the question was put, Rosaleena realised that she did indeed feel unwell.

She excused herself from the table and her mother rose with her, refusing to let her go to her room alone.

Oswald, his mouth full of syllabub, made noises of sympathy, as Sir Uriel watched them leave the room.

"I will send for the doctor if she's no better by the morning," he called after them.

Bridie was nowhere to be seen, so Lady Rosscullen rang for Mary.

Mary helped Rosaleena out of her dress while her mother busied herself with ordering logs for the fire and a warming pan for the bed.

Rosaleena found herself grateful for her mother's attentions.  When at last Lady Rosscullen tucked her into bed and made to depart, Rosaleena reached for her hand.

"Don't go, Mama, till I am asleep," she pleaded.

 "All right, my dear, I will stay."

She laid a comforting hand on her forehead and she closed her eyes.

Her mother's presence seemed to keep her troubled thoughts at bay and in no time at all she was fast asleep.

*

The next morning, however, she woke with a high temperature.  The doctor was called and without hesitation she was confined to bed.

Tossing and turning under the satin sheets, she was plagued with suspicions of a love interest between Bridie and Colonel Joyce.

Her thoughts ran this way and that on the subject.

The Colonel had confessed that he had felt a great urge to see her, Rosaleena.

Why would he say that – or feel that – if he was in love with Bridie? He had enlisted Bridie's aid in bringing Rosaleena to the waterfall, that was all!

But if Bridie was no more than the go-between, why had he kissed her like that on the forehead?

And why did Bridie seem to know so much about the Colonel's past?

Bridie appeared with the excuse that the previous evening she had gone to visit someone in the village, not thinking that Rosaleena would leave the dinner table early.

Dimly she watched Bridie coming and going in the room, stoking the fire or lighting candles as the day waned.

She wanted to engage the maid in conversation, but found that she barely had the strength to issue a command.

At last, however, she struggled up on her elbow to halt Bridie in her tasks.

"When did you – first make the acquaintance – of Colonel Joyce?" she managed to ask.

"Don't you be mentioning that name in this house," Bridie hissed, throwing an anxious look at the door.

Rosaleena fell back on the pillow.

"I would like to know – how you came to be so familiar with the Colonel's – with that gentleman's history – that's all," she said weakly.

Bridie regarded her haughtily.

"I am sure there's a good many things you would like to know, but you'll not hear them from *my* lips."

After that, Rosaleena did not press her.

She longed for news of the Colonel and wondered if Bridie was still in contact with him, but she resolutely refrained from asking the questions out loud.

'He probably does not even know I am ill,' she thought sadly.

*

Then, one afternoon, she woke from a deep sleep to find a bunch of primroses on her pillow.

Bridie was sewing on a chair by the window and so Rosaleena called her over.

"Where did these come from?" she asked.

"I was given them," said Bridie with a meaningful look, "to pass on to you."

Rosaleena's heart leapt as she understood.

"He is still – nearby, then?"

Bridie gave a quick nod.

"He is."

She would say no more. Obviously she was still in contact with him, but Rosaleena found she did not mind.

The flowers spoke volumes. The Colonel knew she was ill and was thinking of her.

That was enough.

Bridie found a vase for the delicate little flowers and set them on the cabinet by the bed.

When they began to fade, Rosaleena pressed one between the pages of her poetry book.

By the end of the week Rosaleena was on her feet again. She yearned to go out, but the weather had taken a turn for the worse and her mother forbade her to leave the house.

It was now that she was once again the subject of unwanted attentions from Oswald.

He had chosen not to visit her whilst she was ill, citing his own propensity to catch colds and Rosaleena was grateful to be spared his presence.

Now, however, he seemed determined to make up for lost time, as he followed her around with an affected lovesick expression on his face.

He resumed trying to prove himself indispensable. He rushed to plump up cushions behind her back, offered to read to her and found reasons to compliment her.

"You look decidedly pretty today, Rosaleena," he said one morning as she descended the stairs towards him.

She stopped a few steps above him and frowned.

"Oswald, I don't! I have no colour in my face, my eyes are dull and my hair duller. I have never looked less pretty in my life."

"Love is blind," responded Oswald cheerfully.

Rosaleena raised her eyes to Heaven.

It did not help to discover that Lady Rosscullen now considered a union between her daughter and Oswald as a *fait accompli*.

"I found some lace in a closet that could be made into a veil," she remarked one evening before the fire.

Rosaleena lowered the book she was reading.

"A veil?"

"Yes, dear. For your marriage to Oswald."

Rosaleena took a deep breath.

"Mama, I have no intention of marrying my cousin, Oswald."

Lady Rosscullen chose to misinterpret her words.

"You need not be worried that he is your cousin. He is not your cousin by blood, my dear."

Rosaleena felt her anger rising.

"I don't care what relation he is to me, so long as he is *not* my husband."

Lady Rosscullen bridled.

"You are a wilful creature, Rosaleena Rosscullen."

Rosaleena stared at the book open in her lap.

"Mama," she asked softly, "why are you so taken with the idea of this match? Is Uncle Uriel now making his influence felt upon you?"

Lady Rosscullen looked uneasy.

"I hope you don't think me as weak as all that."

"Of course not, Mama."

"It's just that – we do owe your uncle a great deal. You have no idea what a support he was after – after I was left a widow with a tiny baby and no inkling of how to run an estate or manage my affairs."

Rosaleena realised that the issue of her marriage to Oswald was destined to be a battle of will between herself and her mother with Uncle Uriel the puppet master.

They were each aroused from their thoughts by the sound of wheels drawing up outside the house.

They listened as someone leapt from a carriage and hammered at the front door. There were voices as the door was opened and then silence.

Lady Rosscullen glanced at the clock on the mantel.

"Whoever could be calling at this hour? It is past eight o'clock and we have yet to dine."

As if on cue, Mary opened the door to announce supper and Lady Rosscullen beckoned her in.

"A visitor has arrived, Mary?"

"Yes, ma'am. I showed him into the dinin' room, since the Master was already at table."

"You should have shown him into the study, to wait there for Sir Uriel," scolded Lady Rosscullen.

Mary looked downcast.

"Sorry, ma'am."

"Well, the harm's done. Rosaleena, let's go in and meet this new guest."

They entered the dining room to find Oswald, Sir Uriel and the guest at the far end of the table.

They all rose as Lady Rosscullen and Rosaleena moved to their seats.

Rosaleena looked at the guest with curiosity.

He was a tall barrel-chested individual with a shock of dun-coloured hair and a beefy red face and he had an insolent air about him.

Sir Uriel introduced him.

"This is Captain Huggins, an acquaintance of mine from many years back. I have invited him to sup with us."

Captain Huggins bared a row of broken teeth.

"Pleased to meet you, ladies."

Rosaleena's blood ran cold at his voice. It was him – the man who had called on her uncle in the dead of night all those weeks ago in London.

With that recognition came yet another memory. It had been from him she had first heard the name 'Kilvarra'!

Sir Uriel gave Lady Rosscullen a significant look.

"Captain Huggins came here to inform us that our fellow is in Ireland."

Knowing that 'our fellow' referred to the Colonel, Rosaleena was immediately alert.

Lady Rosscullen meanwhile had paled.

"W-where in Ireland do you think he is, Captain?"

Captain Huggins ran his tongue over his teeth.

"I've no doubt he'll be hiding out near Rosscullen, your Ladyship, it's where he considers his business to lie."

"His business being the slitting of all our throats, I should not wonder," Sir Uriel observed.

Rosaleena noticed that her uncle's hand shook as he reached for his glass.

Captain Huggins reassured him.

"We'll smoke him out, no fear," he promised. "As you know, there are a few around who won't want him at large. I'll get up a search party at dawn."

Rosaleena listened to this anxiously. Bridie must know what was happening and the sooner the better.

She decided to use her recent illness as an excuse to forego dinner, pleading that she had no appetite and felt tired.

With reluctance her uncle allowed her to leave the table and her mother promised to send her some soup up.

Rosaleena ran swiftly to her room, where she found Bridie turning down the bed.

She looked up in surprise as her Mistress entered.

Rosaleena made sure to close the door fast behind her before hastening over to Bridie.

"The Colonel is discovered," she whispered.

Bridie's face drained of colour.

"How?"

"There is a man here, a Captain Huggins – " began Rosaleena, but Bridie cut her off.

"Captain Huggins. Ha! You need say no more."

She caught up her shawl.

"I must warn the Colonel. I'll go to him tonight. I'll have to find a weapon for myself in case I meet up with that Huggins on the way."

She moved quickly towards the door, then paused on the threshold.

"Thank you," she said softly and was gone.

Staring at the door, Rosaleena now prayed to God that the Colonel would escape the clutches of the odious Captain Huggins.

She was at a loss as to what to do next, so sat down at her dressing table and began with difficulty to unpin her hair. She dared not summon Mary and reveal too soon that Bridie was not in attendance.

She had to give Bridie time to get away.

At last her hair fell around her shoulders in a glossy mass and now she would have to tackle her gown.

As she rose, she heard a sudden commotion from the hall below.

She ran to the door and, opening it, hurried along the passage to the stairwell.

Below she saw Bridie struggling to escape the grip of the one of the stablemen, a brutal looking fellow whom she knew as Peter.

He held the maid easily with one hand, while with his other he had a musket and he was calling for Sir Uriel.

Then Sir Uriel, Oswald and Captain Huggins came out into the hall, Lady Rosscullen hovering in their wake.

"I caught the creature here taking this musket from the gun room," said Peter with an air of triumph.

Sir Uriel went to Bridie and took her chin roughly.

"What did you want this for, young woman?"

"To shoot rabbits," came Bridie's snarling reply.

"Rabbits?" echoed Captain Huggins. "In the dark?"

Bridie gave him a withering look.

"I planned to go out at dawn."

"Did you now?" sneered Captain Huggins. "I'd say it was more than rabbits you were after."

"Sure, why would a lady's maid be goin' huntin' at all?" interjected Peter.

"Let me go! You English-lover!" cried out Bridie, aiming a kick at his shin.

Sir Uriel and Captain Huggins exchanged a look.

"Take her to the cellar to calm down," Sir Uriel told Peter. "The Captain and I will interrogate her later."

Throwing back her head in disdain, Bridie caught sight of Rosaleena watching from above.

Her eyes blazed a message that Rosaleena could not fail to decipher.

'*Save him, save him,*' they silently pleaded.

Rosaleena gave a nod and Bridie looked relieved as her captor hauled her away.

Hurrying to her room, Rosaleena took up her cloak and flung it around her shoulders. She then reached into the wardrobe and retrieved the Colonel's cloak.

Next she opened her bedroom door and listened.

All seemed quiet below.

Gliding swiftly down the stairs, she ran to the front door and drew it carefully open.

With no one to guide her, with neither candle nor lantern to light the way, she must find the waterfall – or the Colonel would fall into the hands of his direst enemies!

# CHAPTER SEVEN

The world seemed as black as pitch as she edged along the path that ran through the kitchen garden.

Dark earth melded into darker sky. Most nights the stars over Rosscullen were bright as silver pins, but tonight they were all hidden, as was the moon.

She had not dared bring a light of any kind in case someone had looked out from the house. The yellow glow would have been visible bobbing through the trees.

She could not run the risk of alerting Sir Uriel or Captain Huggins of her departure.

Rosaleena made her way round to the front of the house. With the building behind her, she knew that she must veer to the left.

She stopped with a tiny cry as something swooped close to her ear. Immediately she glanced back certain that someone must have heard her, but no one stirred.

She felt her way forward again.

It was chill and she was glad of the Colonel's heavy cloak, which she had put on over her own. The two of them created a fearful weight, but she was determined that the Colonel should not continue to suffer the cold.

More by instinct than certainty she came upon the ravine. She hovered at its rim, fearing the steep descent in the dark, but her heart urged her on.

She could almost hear his voice in her ear.

*"They are out for my blood. Though not for the reasons you have been told."*

How she had puzzled over what those reasons must be. Was it something to do with the 'misfortune' that had first driven the Colonel from Ireland?

She had longed to ask Bridie, but had felt too proud after the first rebuff.

She slid her foot over the edge of the ravine and carefully, heart pounding, she made her way down.

It was a long and slow process, but at last she felt the ground even out.

Now she prayed fervently that she would not fall and injure herself whilst crossing the rocky terrain ahead.

As if in answer to her prayer, the moon suddenly sailed majestically out from dark clouds. It was a full moon and shed a plentiful light.

Now she could move with greater speed.

After about half-an-hour she heard the sound of the cascading waters ahead and in another ten minutes she was at the side of the pool.

Wondering how to announce her presence, she felt on the ground for a large stone.

Finding one, she flung it with all her strength into the middle of the pool, hoping that it would make a loud enough splash to be heard above the roaring water.

It did not and in desperation she put her hands to her mouth and called out as loud a 'halloo' as she dared.

Again her voice was drowned by tumbling water.

Hopelessly she sat down on a wet rock and burst into tears. How could she possibly return to the house and tell Bridie that she had failed?

Wiping her eyes on her sleeve, she looked up.

Her heart gave a sudden lurch as she saw a figure seemingly part the curtain of water that fell from the bluff and then he was wading towards her.

It was the Colonel.

She moved eagerly to the edge of the pool to meet him and his face was grave as he drew near.

"You have not come with good news, I am certain," he said.

"No, I have not," she answered, her eyes devouring his features as he stepped out of the pool before her.

"Well?" he demanded.

Rosaleena faltered under his stern gaze.

"A Captain Huggins arrived tonight at Rosscullen. He brought information that you are in Ireland."

Colonel Joyce swore softly.

"Where's Bridie?" he then asked.

"T-they caught her as she was taking a musket from the gunroom. She sent me instead."

The Colonel let out a cry of rage.

"Tell her I'll leave before dawn, but if they touch a hair of her head, they will not live!"

Rosaleena felt plunged into misery.

"Y-you love her so much – then?" she blurted out.

"With my whole being," he replied at once, his jaw clenched. "She is an indelible part of my past?"

Rosaleena was crushed.

Her body shook as she removed his cloak.

"I brought this back for you."

As Rosaleena held out the cloak, he caught hold of her wrist and stayed her arm.

"You have proved yourself your father's daughter tonight," he said in somewhat softened tones. "I will never forget your bravery."

Rosaleena's eyes filled with tears.

"It wasn't bravery – " she began, but the Colonel raised a warning hand.

"Listen!"

Over the rush of the waterfall came another sound.

Dogs, barking with an alarming eagerness.

The Colonel pulled Rosaleena to his breast.

"You must bide with me a while yet," he said, "for our Captain Huggins has set out early to catch his prey."

Rosaleena tried to pull away.

"I c-can't be found here," she began, but her protest was silenced, as without a word the Colonel scooped her up in his arms and re-entered the pool.

She clung fearfully to him as he crossed the pool and crashed through the waterfall.

On the other side he walked up a damp slope and entered a cave that was hidden there under the bluff.

The entrance of the cave was narrow and ran some yards into the rock before opening into a lofty chamber.

Flickering candles revealed a basic but comfortable living space, containing a camp bed, thick blankets and a small table covered with papers.

Rosaleena could not help a surge of jealousy as she imagined Bridie preparing this hideout for him.

This thought set her struggling to be set down, but he grasped her even tighter, as if reluctant to let her go.

"Colonel Joyce!" she called out, but his answer was a soft groan as he buried his face in her hair.

"To have you here with me alone," he murmured, "is an unexpected pleasure. Almost worth the danger!"

Turning her face up to him, Rosaleena was struck by the ardour of his expression.

For a man in love with someone other than herself, he seemed remarkably moved by her.

She remembered her mother's remark that Irishmen were 'wild and unpredictable' and asked herself in alarm if her honour was suddenly at stake.

With a shiver that was half-fear, half-unconscious desire, she entreated him to remember that she was indeed alone with him there in the cave.

"I hope you will prove yourself a gentleman," she finished, feeling a little foolish even as she said it.

The Colonel's mood changed abruptly.

"A gentleman?" he repeated with a sardonic twist to his lip. "How could I be? Haven't you heard we Irish are an infernally barbarous race of men and no woman is safe in our company?"

Mistaking this to mean that he would feel as free to importune her as he had no doubt importuned Bridie, tears started from Rosaleena's eyes.

Seeing this, the Colonel's anger faded.

"Forgive me," he said with remorse. "I have indeed forgotten my manners living in this rough state."

He wiped her tears away before leading her – too stricken to resist – over to the camp bed. There he set her gently down.

He tucked the blanket around her and then moved about the cave quenching various candles with his fingers.

"This cave is pretty deep," he explained, "and the light should not be seen, but I am taking no chances."

He left just one candle burning, which he set beside Rosaleena on the bed.

Then he moved quietly to the mouth of the cave.

The dogs were near.

Hearing their barking, Rosaleena forgot her tears. She was suddenly afraid, wondering what would happen if she was indeed discovered here with the Colonel.

Colonel Joyce returned to her stealthily.

"Don't worry," he said, as if reading her thoughts. "The dogs will not find the cave. If they pick up a scent at the water's edge, it will be assumed that I have been here to swim, but moved on. Nobody knows about this cave, only Bridie, myself and – "

Here the Colonel paused and Rosaleena scanned his face expectantly.

" – and one boyhood friend," he finished.

Rosaleena was surprised that the Colonel should be so acquainted with the estate at Rosscullen as to know the whereabouts of this secret cave, but she said nothing, for she had heard the calls of men in the darkness outside.

She and the Colonel sat there in utter stillness, the Colonel listening closely.

"I would say there are three or four men out there," he murmured after a while.

Rosaleena's heart turned over in her breast as she watched him. His eyes were mesmerising her, glittering like green glass in the flickering light of the one candle.

She saw him stiffen as Captain Huggin's voice rang out loud and clear.

"We'll find you, never fear. You won't escape us, Kilvarra."

*Kilvarra*!

Rosaleena stood up with an astonished cry and the Colonel was at her side at once, his hand clasped roughly to her mouth.

She struggled in his grip, her mind in turmoil.

Kilvarra!

The name of the man who found her father dead. The man whose name her mother could not bear to hear mentioned. The man who was her father's friend and at whose castle Bridie had lived as the gatekeeper's daughter!

Why had the Colonel hidden his true identity from the moment that he and she first met?

The sound of the dogs and the men moved away.

The Colonel – Kilvarra as she now knew him to be – released her.

She shrank back against the chill wall of the cave, watching him as he relit the candles from the one flame.

At last he turned and met her shaken gaze.

"So now you know," he said coolly. "I am the Earl of Kilvarra, although my estate is no more than a bare cave and to speak my name in my country is to risk my life."

"It was you who – found my father – dead!"

The Earl looked grim.

"I did. A day that was cursed under Heaven."

"How – did he die?"

The Earl of Kilvarra hesitated.

"I cannot tell you yet. When the time is right – you will learn."

Bitterness and distrust flooded through Rosaleena, as she realised that yet again her questions were to be met with nothing but a blank wall.

With a loud cry of frustration, she launched herself at him, beating her fists upon his breast.

"I am tired of all these lies and evasions," she cried. "I don't want to stay here any longer. I am leaving now!"

She turned to run towards the cave's entrance, but the Earl caught at her wrists.

"No you don't, my wild cat. I must keep you here a while longer."

Angrily she struggled against him, but his strength prevailed. Soon she could resist no more and then fell exhausted against him.

The beat of his heart sounded faster than her own as she lifted her head and felt his quickening breath.

The next instant he had lost all semblance of self-control.

Catching hold of her hair, he forced her head back, pressing his lips onto hers so ardently that she thought that she would faint with the sudden rush of ecstasy.

She felt her cloak slip from her shoulders, but she did not care.

She did not struggle now, but met his passion with her own.

When he drew his lips away, she arched her back in silent pleading for his kisses to continue. Her body was melting at his touch.

"My darling one," he murmured and in one move caught her swooning body up into his arms.

He carried her back to the camp bed and lay her down as carefully as if she was made of porcelain.

She felt as if his kiss had drawn all her energy and all resistance from her.

She gazed at him, realising that Bridie or no Bridie, she was now powerless to forbid him anything.

Her honour was in his hands.

As if realising this, he did not hold her to him, but knelt in seeming supplication at her side.

Tenderly he wiped away the traces of tears from her cheeks and pushed her curls from her face.

"Rosaleena, my beauty, all that I have hidden from you has been for a good reason. In this country the Earl of Kilvarra is under sentence of death. Until that sentence is removed, I have no right to burden you with the truth or ask from you that which my heart most desires."

Rosaleena reached up a hand to touch his face, even as her eyes half-closed with sudden overwhelming fatigue.

It must be well past midnight and she had not slept for many hours.

The passion that had raced through her fragile body had exhausted her beyond measure.

He caught her hand and his eyelids half closed as he kissed her palm.

"Tell me," Rosaleena asked him drowsily. "Why did you flee – London?"

"Your mother recognised me there," said the Earl in a low voice. "And I knew that I was no longer safe. At the same time your uncle realised that he was no longer safe, for as keenly as he pursues me, I pursue him!"

"But you will not tell me why?"

"No," the Earl smiled. "I will not tell you why yet. I suspected that he would flee to Rosscullen, not thinking I would come here myself."

Rosaleena's eyes flickered open for a moment.

"And did you come here because you are – in love with Bridie?" Her eyes were beginning to close.

The Earl gave a low laugh.

"Never, in all the years it took to make the world, could I feel the same way about her as I feel about you. Is that an answer to please you?"

Rosaleena smiled

"It – pleases me."

The next instant she was asleep.

*

When she awoke some hours later, the candles were burned out and the Earl was gone.

He had before leaving unlaced the very top of her bodice so that she might breathe easier and then covered her with a blanket.

Blushing with pleasure as she remembered all that had passed before she fell asleep, she pushed the blanket away and rose from the bed.

Spying a small mirror she went over to it and stood before it. She caught her own eyes and blushed again.

Her cheeks seemed very pink and her pupils dark.

Was the face there in the glass the face of a young woman in love?

'How can I love the Earl?' she asked herself. 'A man whose name my mother cannot bear to hear? A man who is even now being hunted down by my uncle?'

Turning away from the mirror, she caught sight of a letter, folded and left under a pewter mug on the table.

She read it eagerly.

"*My Rosaleena, I shall carry the memory of your kiss with me until we meet again. Read and then destroy this letter, for your own safety if not mine.*

*Your own Kilvarra.*"

Rosaleena was glad he had slipped away to safety as she kissed the letter and then stood hesitating. She knew that she should obey him, but it was more than she could bear to do away with this, her first love letter from him.

At last she folded it up, put it into her bosom and then, catching up her cloak, she left the cave.

It was nearly dawn outside.

She stared out through the sheet of water that hid the cave from view and she did not relish passing through it, but there was no choice.

She slid down the slope and then, head bent, rushed into the waterfall and out the other side.

She was thigh deep in the pool and gasped in shock to find it ice cold at that hour of the morning and, by the time she had waded to the other side, the lower part of her gown was drenched.

This slowed her progress back to the house, but she reached it before too many of its inhabitants were awake.

The shutters were still closed of her uncle's and her mother's rooms and she could be sure that Oswald would not yet be out of bed.

But the servants would be about their business and she must take care to avoid their inquisitive eyes.

There was a door at the side of the house that led into the laundry room. She would try that.

The door was locked so she rattled the latch angrily but it would not give and she was about to turn away when suddenly it was opened from within.

'*I am discovered*,' she thought in consternation.

Then with relief and some surprise, she saw that it was Bridie who stood before her.

Bridie put a finger to her lips and drew her in.

"I thought you had been locked up in the cellar," exclaimed Rosaleena as Bridie closed the door behind her.

"I was," said Bridie in a low voice. "Mrs. Lynch released me an hour ago."

"Mrs. Lynch!" Rosaleena was startled.

Bridie nodded.

"Mrs. Lynch is on our side. But tell me, is *he* safe?"

"Yes, the Earl of Kilvarra is safe."

"Oh!" Bridie let out her breath. "So you know?"

"I know."

They stood for a moment, each in contemplation of the other as Rosaleena grew uncomfortable, imagining that Bridie felt the change in relations between her and the Earl.

"Where are you off to?" she asked at last, gesturing to the bundle of provisions in Bridie's arms.

Bridie gave a wry smile.

"Do you think I'd stay here to be interrogated by your uncle and Captain Huggins? I am to join the Earl."

Rosaleena, recalling his revelation that '*never, in as many years as it took to make the world*,' would he love Bridie as he loved her, made her feel sorry for her maid.

Yet at the same time she was full of hurt that it was Bridie and not herself who would join him in exile.

"Tell him – I am home and safe," she said to Bridie.

Bridie gave a short nod and was gone.

Rosaleena then tiptoed to her room, encountering nobody but Mary, who stared in surprise at her wet gown.

"I went out for an early walk and – and fell into the stream," said Rosaleena by way of explanation.

"Sure, you've only just come out of your sickbed," Mary reminded Rosaleena.

"I know," said Rosaleena as meekly as she could. "But I do so love to be out as the sun is rising."

"I wouldn't care if I never saw the dawn again," grumbled Mary. "I was called down early, having to take off that Captain Huggins's boots and prepare his porridge."

"When – when did he come in?" asked Rosaleena carelessly.

"About three o'clock in the morning."

Three o'clock! Rosaleena's mind raced. That was soon after he had been at the waterfall with the dogs. It meant he would not have been in the vicinity when the Earl actually left.

"He seemed awful angry," Mary continued. "He didn't find what he was lookin' for anyways."

Her expression was innocent and yet Rosaleena was sure that Mary knew her words were very welcome and she understood that she could implicitly trust the girl.

"Mary," she said softly. "I would be very grateful if you said nothing about seeing me coming in so early this morning."

"I just wouldn't give anyone the satisfaction."

"Thank you," said Rosaleena. She was about to go when a thought struck her. "Would you be so kind as to bring me breakfast at about nine o'clock? Bridie has – left Rosscullen for good."

Mary barely blinked.

"I will, miss. Cook made some farls last night. I'll bring them up with some honey."

'Well,' mused Rosaleena as she went to her room. 'The whole household seems to be in league with Bridie. But I don't care, for that means they are in league with me too – and the Earl.'

Reaching her room, she closed the door carefully behind her and began to undo her bodice and skirt.

Not troubling to pull on her nightshift, she slipped with a sigh into the comfort of her own soft bed.

Her hand rested on the Earl's letter, which she had transferred from her bodice to her thin under-chemise.

She was wondering where the Earl was now and how Bridie hoped to find him.

He had acknowledged Bridie as '*an indelible part of his past*' and Rosaleena assumed that he was alluding to the fact that he had known Bridie as a child.

She believed now that the Earl was not in love with Bridie, but was convinced that Bridie was in love with the Earl, for she was taking a great risk to join him.

Rosaleena could not close her eyes, but a vision of the Earl as she had seen him last rose before her. His green eyes full of wild longing and a lock of his dark hair falling over his face as he bent towards her.

He could have ravished her there and he had not. All Irishmen were not untrustworthy, as her mother said!

At the thought of her mother, her heart sank. She did not care if her relationship with the Earl should offend her uncle and Oswald, but she did care about the pain it would inflict on her mother.

Why the Earl should be so scared because he had happened to come upon the body of his friend, her father, Rosaleena could not fathom out, but she knew her mother's character, which was weak and prey to superstitions.

'The Earl must have been a very young man when he was my father's friend,' she reflected, for he was the younger and her father was barely nineteen when he died.

She chided herself for once thinking that the Earl was too old for her. He seemed to her now so far the most superior gentleman she had ever met that she could not imagine what crime he had committed and for which he was being hunted down like a mad dog.

'If he never proves his innocence of this mysterious crime, I don't care, I will marry him and go abroad with him, if needs must.'

Dreaming about the Earl, she fell into a half-sleep.

How long it lasted she did not know, but it seemed only a matter of minutes before she started from her pillow, awakened by loud footsteps in the passage outside.

Before she could reach for her dressing gown, her door slammed open and Oswald burst unceremoniously in.

"H-how dare you enter my room without so much as a knock!" admonished Rosaleena.

"And how dare you lie there looking as if butter wouldn't melt in your mouth," he squawked, "when you know full well that Bridie has escaped and with your help, I am quite certain."

"I had nothing to do with it," she cried truthfully.

"I don't believe you!" screamed Oswald.

Angrily Rosaleena sprang up from her bed and then ordered him from her room.

"I won't leave without you," he retorted. "You are coming with me to explain yourself to my father and the Captain."

With that Oswald grasped her arm so tightly that she cried out in pain.

Wrenching herself away from him, the letter from the Earl fell from her chemise and fluttered to the floor.

Seeing it, Oswald made a lunge and picked it up.

Despite Rosaleena's wild protestations, he held her at bay with his free hand while he read its contents.

When he looked up, his face was black with fury.

"And my foolish father brought you here precisely to avoid this! So now you know that 'Colonel Joyce' is the Earl of Kilvarra, a liar and a traitor, someone who your mother hates and yet you allow him to make overtures to you. Well, Papa and your mother shall know all."

This time, Rosaleena could not free herself from his grip. He dragged her after him, down the stairs, past the startled Mary with her breakfast tray and into the drawing room, shouting all the while for his father.

Rosaleena, flung uncivilly into a chair, sat shaking under his baleful gaze.

Sir Uriel flew in, tightening the cord of his dressing gown, with Lady Rosscullen just behind him, pale in her morning gown.

Rosaleena grew sullen as she saw the Captain come next. He had not taken off his clothes, it seemed, as his breeches were muddy from his night time quest.

"What is going on here, Oswald?" demanded Sir Uriel. "Are we not now exercised quite enough with the disappearance of this Bridie creature?"

"Read this," Oswald said, thrusting the letter at his father.

Sir Uriel read it. His face blazed with anger as he handed it silently on to Lady Rosscullen.

Her reaction was more extreme still. Staggering as if struck, she groped for the support of a chair as the letter fell from her hands and lay open on the fireside rug.

"How is it possible," she now moaned. "How is it possible that you defy us like this?"

Rosaleena summoned all her strength.

Legs trembling, she rose to confront her mother.

"Mama," she said, trying to stop her voice shaking, "I do not intend to defy you. But there is something you must know, because I cannot hide it from you any longer. I have fallen in love with the Earl of Kilvarra."

The scream that her mother gave in answer chilled Rosaleena to the bone.

"Foolish child," she cried, her eyes large and wild with despair. "Foolish child, to fall in love with the man who murdered your father!"

# CHAPTER EIGHT

For a moment, Rosaleena could not believe that she had heard aright.

"M-murdered?"

Lady Rosscullen sank into an armchair, hand to her forehead.

"Uriel – you enlighten her.  Please do."

Rosaleena turned terrified eyes to her uncle.

He gestured for her to sit, but she could not move. She was frozen to the spot.  It was Oswald who took her elbow and guided her to a chair by the window.

Sir Uriel began,

"In the year 1798 I arrived at Rosscullen House to stay with my step-sister Constance and her young husband Lord Rosscullen.  The couple had just had their first and, as it sadly turned out, only child – you, Rosaleena.

"It was a time of political upheaval in Ireland with rebels attacking those they considered representative of the British Establishment such as landlords and the aristocracy. It was no surprise to me when one evening, the carriage in which I and Lord Rosscullen were driving was attacked.

"Your father was nothing if not a very brave man and between the two of us the attackers were repulsed.  It was a hard lesson and our lives were in constant danger.

"I therefore felt it right for me to press upon my host, your father, the importance of him making a will and appointing a Guardian for his newly-born daughter.  For once – he was a headstrong fellow sometimes – your father followed my advice. He then made a will, nominating as Trustees and Guardians both myself and his own lifelong but younger friend – the Earl of Kilvarra."

Rosaleena raised her eyes at the sound of the name.

"I had never trusted the Earl," Sir Uriel continued. "His views were too liberal for my tastes and I suspected he harboured a secret admiration for the rebels. But even I could not have guessed the depths to which the Earl was prepared to sink to express his political beliefs.

"He often stayed with his friends at nearby Scarrig House, friends who were equally suspect to my mind. One day he invited your father and myself to join him in a hunt.

"Rather than our riding all the way to Scarrig, he suggested we meet at a half-way point in Magully Woods. Your father agreed. I wish to Heaven he had not or that I had voiced my concerns at the idea of waiting at such an isolated spot when there were so many villains abroad.

"But I was silent and have rued the day ever since."

Sir Uriel paused as Lady Rosscullen let out a wail and buried her face in her hands.

Rosaleena could not find it in herself to go to her mother. Neither her body nor her mind were her own to command, such weakness of spirit engulfed her.

Her uncle's cold and calm voice fell like a hammer on her, demolishing step by step her dream of happiness.

He continued,

"The day of the hunt turned out to be grey and dull. Lord Rosscullen and I rode out early. And just before we reached the meeting place, we were attacked again. This time the attackers were greater in number.

"Your father was mortally wounded. I managed to escape, but not before I recognised one of them. It was the Earl of Kilvarra and it was he who fired the fatal shot."

Rosaleena felt as if an icy hand had tightened about her heart.

"I managed to escape and fortunately encountered a Militia patrol passing nearby and convinced them to return with me to the scene of the crime.

"Approaching stealthily, they caught the Earl in the process of stealing my dead friend's fob watch. The Earl, armed with his musket, resisted arrest and escaped."

Sir Uriel stopped a moment before continuing,

"As we discovered later, the Earl fled that night to France. Since this was the preferred destination of many failed rebel leaders, it was enough to link him to various rebellions all over Ireland that year and that suggested a political motive for the killing of his friend."

"I – cannot – believe it," whispered Rosaleena, sick to the depths of her soul.

She meant that all she had heard was too much to take in, but Sir Uriel took it differently and frowned.

"You cannot believe it?" he snapped and signalled to his son. "Oswald, call in Captain Huggins."

Captain Huggins must have been lurking nearby as Oswald merely had to open the door and beckon him in.

Rosaleena, eyes low, stared at the Captain's muddy boots as he entered.

"Captain Huggins," said Sir Uriel. "Would you be so kind as to confirm the events I have just been describing to my niece? I think you know of what I speak."

"I do indeed, Sir Uriel," he replied.

"I was Captain of a local Militia patrol that day and we encountered Sir Uriel here in a state of distress. He told us that he had been attacked and led us back to the scene.

"There we came across a really horrible sight. The young Lord Rosscullen with a bullet in his chest and his killer rifling through his bloodied shirt for his watch."

"And did you know who it was?" demanded Sir Uriel, his eyes on Rosaleena's crushed form.

"I did. It was the Earl of Kilvarra."

With a cry of despair, Rosaleena covered her face with her hands.

Sir Uriel was not done yet.

"The Irish are a vengeful nation," he went on. "The Earl as a Trustee knew the contents of Lord Rosscullen's will and the date on which you, Rosaleena, came into your estate. In the guise of a Colonel Joyce, confident that after a lapse of twenty-one years he would not be recognised by myself or your mother, he had made his way to London to attempt to inveigle his way into your affections and so lay claim to your fortune."

"No, *no*," moaned Rosaleena.

"And when he was discovered there," persisted Sir Uriel, "recognised at last by your mother, did he abandon his attempt and return to France? No. He just recklessly followed us to Ireland, where his face is better known and the risk of detection so much greater, and persevered in his courtship.

"He even dared admit, as this note reveals, that he is in fact the Earl of Kilvarra, confident that we had not divulged his wickedness to you. No doubt his plan was to abduct you and marry you before you had learned the truth, then whisk you and your fortune abroad. Was there ever a greater blackguard in existence?"

"No more," wailed Rosaleena clasping her hands to her ears. "No more!"

Lady Rosscullen gestured to Sir Uriel that enough was enough and for once he heeded her.

"Come on, Captain Huggins," he said with a hint of triumph in his voice. "We have done what we had to do."

He beckoned to Oswald to follow and they left the room, Oswald casting a concerned look at Rosaleena.

She was weeping silently, tears of despair coursing down her cheeks.

The man whose lips had devoured hers – the man in whose arms she had languished – the man whose words had made her swoon – was the man who had murdered her own father!

Lady Rosscullen had the sensitivity to remain silent and at a distance.

For a while just the sound of Rosaleena's sobs rent the air and gradually these subsided.

The house then seemed eerily silent, as though no one moved or spoke or went about their business.

Lady Rosscullen stirred.

"Rosaleena?" she ventured.

She raised lifeless eyes to her mother's face.

"Why was I never told the truth about my father's death?" she asked.

Lady Rosscullen stumbled over her reply.

"I myself could – could hardly b-bear up under the knowledge. How then could I burden my only child with it? Better, far better, not to discuss the matter."

"Better for you, perhaps," said Rosaleena bitterly, "but not for me. Had I always known the truth – then the instant I discovered Colonel Joyce to be – none other than the murdering Earl, my heart would have been on guard."

Lady Rosscullen's hand flew to her breast in alarm.

"Rosaleena – he has not taken advantage of you?"

She stared with a certain coldness at her mother.

"In an emotional sense he has, yes," she said. "But he has not lain a finger on me, even though – even though he had – the opportunity."

She turned her face away from her mother's relief.

'She does not care at all if my heart is broken,' she thought miserably. 'She only cares to hear that my honour is still intact.'

Lady Rosscullen blew her nose.

"Daughter, I take it from this letter that you have been meeting with the Earl in secret. I hope it is truly in secret and that nobody besides ourselves knows about it."

"Bridie knows."

Lady Rosscullen looked uneasy.

"An employee is not to be trusted. She is likely to gossip. No doubt she would take pleasure in destroying your reputation. My dear, the sooner you are married the better."

"Married?" repeated Rosaleena with a sudden hard laugh. "To the Earl, do you mean?"

Lady Rosscullen regarded her sharply.

"You know that is precisely what I do *not* mean. No, I mean you must now seriously consider the interest that Oswald has shown in you. Heaven knows, if all this business with the Earl has not discouraged him, nothing ever will. There is a steady heart to sustain you through the vicissitudes of life."

A steady heart! The vicissitudes of life! Rosaleena turned and gazed out of the window.

A faltering sun had risen through the dark clouds, the tall pine trees swayed in an early morning breeze and the rocky incline of the ravine still glistened with dew.

The dew was like her tears. It would dry as the day advanced and her pain would lessen with time.

Meanwhile, why not marry Oswald? She had no fight left to oppose the match. Might as well he as another, was all she thought. At least he was who he said he was.

"All right, Mama," she said wearily. "I accept."

"What did you say?" Lady Rosscullen now sounded excited.

"I said, all right. I will accept Oswald's proposal."

Lady Rosscullen clapped her hands.

"Your uncle will be so pleased."

"I hope Oswald will be pleased too."

"What? Oh, he will be ecstatic. I must go and tell Sir Uriel."

She rose, smoothing her gown and patting her head as if about to be presented at court.

"Will you accompany me, my dear?"

"No, you go, Mama. I would like to be alone here."

If Lady Rosscullen was disturbed by her daughter's subdued tones, she did not show it.

"Well," she said briskly. "I will do as you ask me. We will all convene at lunch. I am sure that Sir Uriel will want to open a bottle or two of champagne in celebration."

Lady Rosscullen departed.

For a long time, Rosaleena remained where she was on the hard wooden chair and half-turned to the window. The scene beyond the glass soothed her tormented mind and despite all that she had suffered in this place, she loved it. London was not only a distant world to her it was a colder world.

She hoped that Oswald would allow her to live here at Rosscullen. In fact, she promised herself, that she would make it a condition of her marriage that he does so. He can go to London whenever he likes after all.

Rising at last, she paced the room. Every article in it was hers, but after her marriage, it would all belong to Oswald too.

Well, that would not matter, as long as he agreed to leave her here to enjoy it.

At last she paused before the gold mirror above the mantel. She examined her features with a cold detachment, seeing that her eyes were without lustre, her cheeks were without colour.

It was the face of someone utterly disillusioned.

With her fingers she traced the contour of her lips, shuddering to think that they had welcomed the kiss of a man who, had she but known it, was her mortal enemy.

A betrayer of friendship, a black-hearted villain of the lowest order, a greedy cheat and a heartless murderer.

Yet even as she condemned the Earl, Rosaleena's heart faltered at the thought of Oswald's lips on hers.

\*

In her mother's faded wedding dress Rosaleena sat numbly at the side of her uncle.

The wheels of the carriage that bore them to the local Church rattled over the small stones of the road.

Sir Uriel was silent, his gloved hands folded on his knee, his high-crowned hat shielding his face.

Rosaleena had no desire to speak with him. He had been unable to disguise his triumph at her capitulation and she suspected that this day was the culmination of all his ambitions for Oswald.

What it was to Oswald she could only guess. He had seemed almost too relieved to grant her wish that she live mainly in Ireland, while he spent his time in London.

The very thought of Oswald's arms about her made her feel miserable. He had already demanded evidence of her affection in the form of several stolen kisses, which had left her feeling strangely numb.

And how would it be when she must share his bed tonight?

Rosaleena repressed a shudder and turned her face to the carriage window, where rain streamed steadily down the glass.

Once the wedding date was set she had tried hard to adopt the demeanour of a happy bride-to-be, but it seemed that she convinced no one.

Mary heard the news with eyes lowered and was barely able to murmur her congratulations.

Mrs. Lynch looked positively downcast. There was no excited bustle in the house. If anything, the atmosphere became silent and sombre, as if in anticipation of a funeral.

Even Lady Rosscullen had not evinced the pleasure Rosaleena had expected.

When she took her wedding dress out of its trunk, along with desiccated sprigs of lavender, she had sat back on her heels with a sudden sigh.

"Mine was a love match!" she said.

Rosaleena tried to keep her voice steady.

"So you acknowledge that mine is not, Mama?"

Her mother seemed reluctant to answer.

"I pursued the course – I thought best."

"Best?" repeated Rosaleena. "For whom?"

"For you, my dear."

Rosaleena gave a hollow laugh.

"Don't you mean, best for you to have some peace from my uncle? Best for my uncle to have his ambitions fulfilled?"

Tears filled Lady Rosscullen's eyes.

"Don't torment me so, Rosaleena. I do declare that you are an – an ungrateful girl."

'And here I am flying into the deadly flame of a marriage without love,' thought Rosaleena as the carriage bowled along.

Would it have been better to remain the dupe of the heartless Earl of Kilvarra?

'No, a thousand times no,' she cried out to herself silently. 'To deliver myself into hands that were covered with blood, my own father's blood?'

*Impossible*!

The carriage now began to rock as the horses for no apparent reason suddenly stepped up their pace. Sir Uriel caught hold of the leather strap of the door on his side.

"What the devil – " he began, when it stopped with a lurch that threw him and Rosaleena forward violently.

The door on Rosaleena's side was wrenched open with such force that she cried out in fright.

The figure of a masked man reached in, caught her about the waist and hauled her out.

She had time to notice two other masked figures with muskets before she was hoisted onto her abductor's shoulder.

She kicked and screamed, but to no avail.

She heard Sir Uriel call for help, but knew that his words might as well have been thistledown blowing in the wind, as the carriage had been stopped half-way between the house and the village with no one within earshot.

She was then carried swiftly to a waiting horse and thrown across the saddle. Her abductor leapt up behind her and reached for the reins.

"Away!" he cried to his comrades in muffled tones as behind them she heard her uncle's furious voice.

"You'll hang for this, Kilvarra!"

Hearing her uncle name her abductor, she cried out again. She tried to slide from the saddle, but her abductor placed a firm hand on her back and held her on.

"Tsk, tsk, and after all the trouble I took!" he said jovially.

His was indeed the voice of the Earl!

She wriggled with anger, but had to abandon any attempt to escape as the Earl's horse broke into a gallop.

Her mind turned and turned, like mixture stirred in a pudding bowl.

Why had the Earl abducted her and what were his intentions? Where was he taking her? How long before Sir Uriel could raise the alarm?

What would happen then? Did the Earl intend to ransom her?

She opened her eyes and quickly closed them again. The ground was racing by, clods of mud thrown up by the horse's pounding hoofs.

"Whoa!"

Flooded with relief, she heard the Earl call out the command to halt.

He now leapt from the saddle and then swung her down. She stood still for a moment like someone feeling themselves on firm ground after weeks at sea.

At last, feeling steadier, she opened her eyes.

She was in a clearing of a forest of pines. Before her stood a small trap, the horse in its shaft cropping the grass. She did not recognise the driver's face.

She turned her head to meet the gaze of the Earl.

"My apologies for the rough ride you have had so far," he said. "I hope you will find the rest of the journey a little more comfortable."

Rosaleena surveyed him haughtily.

"I have no intention of travelling on with you," she declared.

The Earl gave a grim smile.

"And I have no intention of going on without you."

"Then we have reached an impasse!"

The Earl gave a signal and she heard the click of a musket from behind her.

"You are not in a position to refuse my request," said the Earl politely.

Rosaleena glared at him balefully before crossing to the trap and climbing in. There was a blanket on the seat, which she drew about her.

The trap set off, the Earl's men falling in behind. The Earl himself rode on ahead at such a pace that soon he was lost to view.

Now that she had recovered from the shock of the abduction, she found herself growing cold with fury.

Obviously, either Mary or Mrs. Lynch had kept the Earl apprised of all that was going on at Rosscullen, which was how he had learned that she was to be married today.

The one thing they could not have told him was that she had discovered his invidious role in her father's death.

The road was uneven and, although she was at least upright, she felt every jolt run through her body.

They travelled on for at least two hours through the pine forest and then the land became wilder and rockier.

The road began to ascend and soon the view was hidden in swirls of mist.

Rosaleena hugged the blanket about her body.

She could not help thinking that, if the Earl had not abducted her, she would by now be the wife of Oswald.

*Mrs. Oswald Reece.* Her lips moved silently to pronounce the name as a sense of relief flooded through her.

A howling wind suddenly struck up, blowing the mist away and opening out the vista.

Rosaleena then gasped as she saw ahead the grim ramparts of an old castle loom up.

The trap drove in under an archway and pulled up in a deserted courtyard.

She scrambled from the trap and looked about. The castle seemed to have fallen into rack and ruin.

The wind whistled through gaping roofs and blind windows. Rooks flew to and fro above the ravished walls.

Only one tall stone tower seemed intact. The driver pointed with his whip at a door open at its base.

There was no sign of the Earl, although his horse stood tethered to a nearby post.

She gathered up her skirts and made for the door.

She then climbed a narrow winding stairway that seemed to go on forever. Through arrow slits she glimpsed dark mountains rising up on all sides.

At the very top of the stairs there was a room set in the roof of the tower. It was a large space with latticed windows on all sides.

Logs crackled in a marble hearth. A thick white fur lay draped over a four-poster bed and on a plain pine table stood a flagon of wine and platters of bread and cheese.

Standing at the window with his back to the room was the Earl.

"Come on in," he said without turning his head.

Rosaleena stood resolutely in the open doorway.

"Why have you brought me to this forsaken place?" she demanded.

He turned and parried with a question of his own,

"Why have you proved so fickle in so short a time? Was I mistaken to believe that you had pledged your heart to me and no one else?"

Rosaleena regarded him scornfully.

"What a fool you must be to believe that I would pledge my heart to the man who murdered my father."

The Earl froze.

Then, with a curse, he strode over to her and caught her about the neck.

Tilting her head up, he stared icily at her.

"What do you call me, madam?"

"Murderer, murderer," repeated Rosaleena.

The Earl drew in his breath.

"You have lain against my breast. You have felt my lips on yours. Yet you believe me capable of murder?"

"Yes," came her reply. "A thousand times, *yes*!"

The Earl's eyes blazed and he tightened his grip, before bringing his lips down on hers.

His kiss was rough, passionate, angry and wild.

Rosaleena struggled against him. At last she pulled away, panting for breath and then the Earl whispered,

"I could ravish you now, Rosaleena, here before the fire, without your consent. What is such an act to a man after he has committed murder? It could not stain his soul any more, could it, my darling?"

Rosaleena then broke free from his grip.

"Your soul is black as the soul of the Devil," she cried chokingly. "I could believe anything of you, for what are you but a – wild Irishman, without mercy and without conscience! What did you want of me when you kissed me in London and when you held me in your arms in your lair behind the waterfall? What do you want of me now?"

The Earl answered very softly.

"Do you not know, Rosaleena?"

Rosaleena retaliated in fury.

"You have no right to call me Rosaleena or darling. I hate you! By what right do you abduct me and bring me here? On my wedding day of all days?"

The Earl fell deathly still.

"Forgive me, madam," he said at last. "I thought that you were being forced to marry that simpering fool. I did not realise you welcomed the union."

Rosaleena lifted her head proudly.

"Rather marry a fool than – than a butcher."

The Earl's features hardened to stone and he moved to the door.

"Where are you going?" she cried. "You surely do not intend to keep me here?"

"I most surely do," said the Earl. "Simply to save you from making the gravest mistake of your life. Please consider yourself as my honoured guest. As you see," and here he gestured to the fire and the bed, "we have tried to make it as comfortable as possible for you."

The door was closed behind him before Rosaleena could think to ask who he meant by 'we'.

She heard the key turn in the lock and, rushing to the door, pounded it with her fists, but to no avail.

She was a prisoner.

# CHAPTER NINE

The hours passed and not a soul came near her.

Rosaleena paced the room like a caged animal, her heart raging against the murderous Earl.

She assumed that she must be at his ancestral home, Kilvarra Castle, and this gave her a degree of reassurance. Her uncle would guess that the Earl had brought her here and so it would surely not be long before she was rescued.

Round and round her prison she went, pausing now and then to peer out of one of the numerous windows.

As afternoon wore on into dusk, she began to throw longing looks towards the food that lay on the table. She had determined to accept nothing from the Earl, but at last hunger conquered her will.

Ravenous, she fell on the bread and cheese and then drank a goblet of wine and, feeling somewhat restored, she set herself down on the stool before the fire.

She threw more logs on the fire. Wisps of smoke made their way up the flue and, watching them, her eyes began to close. It had been a long day and she was tired.

She made her way to the bed where, after peeling off her gown, she curled up in her shift under the large fur.

Before long she fell into an exhausted asleep.

She was awakened by the sound of the key turning in the lock.

From beneath the fur she watched as someone with a lantern entered, relocked the door and then tiptoed across to lay something on the table.

Rosaleena sat up quickly and the intruder turned.

It was Bridie.

"Hello, Rosaleena," said Bridie coolly.

Rosaleena regarded her with contempt.

"I would say 'hello Bridie,' but I am sure that is not – your real name."

Bridie smiled.

"Indeed it is not! My real name is Geraldine. It would not have been politic to call myself by my real name at Rosscullen."

Rosaleena scowled.

"I suppose you agreed to be a party to my kidnap – because you are in love with the Earl?"

"Not if he was the last man on earth could I be in love with him!"

Rosaleena raised an eyebrow in disbelief.

"You really don't care for him?"

"Oh, I do!" came the cheerful reply, "but I could never give him my heart in the way you mean. How could I, when he is my own brother?"

Rosaleena gaped in astonishment.

"Your – your brother?"

The first time she had laid eyes on Geraldine she had thought that something about her was familiar. Now she realised what it was. She had the same dark locks, the same high brow and the same arrogant air as the Earl.

But why had his sister become a maid?

Geraldine seemed to read her thoughts.

"I took up employment at Rosscullen so that I could help my brother."

"Help him? How?"

Geraldine's eyes betrayed thinly veiled amusement.

"He wanted to keep abreast of what befell you and, of course, of what progress your uncle made in trying to track him down!"

Rosaleena considered this.

"You took a great risk," she said, almost wistfully.

Geraldine gave a toss of her head.

"What had I to lose? The loss of his reputation was also the loss of mine. Although I was a child when he was forced to flee, my family and I paid for his misfortune too."

Now Rosaleena bridled.

"*Misfortune,* you call it?"

"I do, and what would you call it, Rosaleena?"

"I call it murder."

Geraldine gave a sad shake of her head.

"My parents went to the grave convinced that time would prove my brother's innocence. And time *will* prove it to you as well to as the world."

"Time?" scoffed Rosaleena.

Geraldine's eyes took on a faraway look.

"The time it takes to find the men – who know the truth and persuade them to speak"

Rosaleena's gaze narrowed suspiciously.

"What men?"

"The men who carried out the attack during which your father was shot."

She shrank into the fur and stared at Geraldine, who gestured wearily that she had brought in her supper.

"I am not at all hungry," said Rosaleena petulantly.

"Please yourself."

Geraldine moved towards the door, but Rosaleena detained her.

"Am I at Kilvarra Castle?"

Geraldine laughed.

"Do you take us for fools? No, you are at Bannaboy Tower, the home of cousins of ours, who helped to rescue you today."

"It was not rescue," snapped Rosaleena stubbornly.

Geraldine's lip curled sardonically.

"Was it not? Well, I'll believe you if you lie in that bed tonight wishing that you were in the arms of Oswald Reece!"

With that Geraldine moved swiftly to the door, the key in her hand.

Rosaleena made a move to snatch at the key and Geraldine swung round.

"Don't even think about it. One of my cousins is waiting outside the door."

She unlocked the door, went out and then slammed it behind her.

Rosaleena stared, speechless and confused.

After a moment, she lay down again, ignoring the enticing smell of the food Geraldine had brought her.

The wind moaned in the chimney and the windows rattled in their frames.

Rosaleena tossed and turned, haunted by Bridie's – Geraldine's – words.

Angry as she was, she had to admit that Geraldine was right. She was relieved beyond all measure not to be yielding her body up to Oswald Reece tonight.

At the same time she refused to believe that the Earl was innocent as his sister had claimed. To believe that would be to believe that her own uncle had lied to her and that was unthinkable.

The fire had died down but suddenly she was aware of the flicker of a candle in the room.

Peering out from her bed, she saw the Earl seated by the fire, a candle at his feet and his head in his hands.

The sound of the wind had covered his entrance.

Rosaleena cowered, fearfully imagining that he had come to carry out his earlier threat of ravishing her.

He gave a loud sigh and Rosaleena held her breath.

The next instant her heart lurched with alarm as he rose to his feet and strode over to the bed.

Eyes tight shut she felt the warmth of the candle as he brought it close to her face.

After a moment and despite herself, her eyes then fluttered involuntarily open to meet his.

"Ah," he said sadly as she regarded him, "if I was only the man you think I am, Rosaleena, what might I not claim of you now? I could make you mine for all time."

"You – would not dare," breathed Rosaleena.

The Earl's jaw clenched.

"Not dare? By Heaven, you tempt me. Tempt me to try you with my love – a wilder kind of love than you would ever find with that fool you were about to marry."

So near were his lips to hers, so near his flesh, that Rosaleena shivered.

Even as her heart hardened towards him, her body trembled with weakness and she struggled in a torturous web of desire and hate.

"You would have my b-body, but never have my heart," she cried truthfully.

The Earl's brow darkened.

"I returned to England to clear my name in the eyes of the world. But from the moment I met you I cared only to clear it in your eyes."

Rosaleena, forgetting that she was dressed only in her shift, knelt up in anger.

"Clear your name?" she cried. "How can you clear your name when you are guilty?"

For a moment he did not reply. His pupils flared as he took in the sight of Rosaleena, the fur fallen from her shoulders and the shift clinging to every curve of her body.

Then he forced himself to turn away.

"I am an innocent man," he said huskily. "But I cannot – will not – tell you the truth of what I know until I can furnish proof. Without that proof truth is nothing but a shape-shifter."

"Shape-shifter?" repeated Rosaleena.

"In Irish legend, a shape-shifter is a person capable of changing their image at will. They can become a cat, a dog, a tree. And that is what truth is like, until you can pin it down for good, so that everyone sees the same thing."

"What would you know of truth?" she demanded scornfully, "who has lied to me since the beginning?"

The Earl sighed.

"How could I reveal my true identity to you when I was known to your mother as the man who had killed her husband? Recognised as the Earl, I would have had no chance at all to help you."

"H-help me?" stammered Rosaleena.

"Yes, help you. I don't confess to knowing exactly *who* killed your father, but when I heard in France that Sir Uriel Reece was taking his Guardianship of yourself and your fortune to heart, I began to understand *why*. For the sake of old loyalties, I felt I should be at hand to rescue you should his plans prove nefarious.

"I was not, of course, free to return to England while the war waged on and then when the war was over I was delayed by a personal matter that I had to wind up – "

Rosaleena interrupted him with scorn.

"Oh! You mean – a woman?"

The Earl smiled sardonically.

"You cannot imagine, young lady, that any soldier, and an Irish soldier too, should deny himself the pleasures of female company? I was abroad, for a very long time."

"I can imagine," replied Rosaleena haughtily, "that your 'personal matters' were many."

"I am not a man to do things in half measures, for sure," he said with a flicker of amusement.

"And that includes *murder*, does it not?"

The Earl stood as if struck.

"Will nothing convince you?" he asked at last.

"Nothing!" Rosaleena's look was icy.

"Your heart is turned against me?"

"For ever."

The Earl's features turned to stone before her eyes.

"That is a pity, Miss Rosscullen. For I had decided that the only way to save you from marrying Mr. Oswald Reece is to marry you myself."

Rosaleena was incredulous.

"Is that – why you brought me here?"

The Earl inclined his head.

"I have a Priest on hand. My sister and my cousins could be witnesses."

"It's just as my uncle has said," Rosaleena cried in fury. "You intend to marry me and claim my fortune."

"That is certainly a strategy that your uncle would appreciate, since it is his own. With the minor difference that it is his son who would do the marrying while he, your uncle, did the claiming."

Rosaleena clapped her hands to her ears.

"I will not hear any more. I will never marry you. You disgust me! I hope they catch you and hang you from the highest tree in Ireland!"

The Earl flinched.

"I am almost beginning to hope that they do," he murmured, before moving away.

Rosaleena leapt from the bed.

"You will let me go?" she demanded.

The Earl took the key from the outside lock of the door and threw it to Rosaleena. It clattered to the floor.

"You are at liberty, madam," he said. "But, if you think to bring the full force of the law down upon us here, be warned. I will see Sir Uriel Reece swing first."

And then he was gone.

*

As the Earl's footsteps faded, Rosaleena stooped to pick up the key. She did not need it, since he had left the door swinging open.

Warily she dressed and then ran down the stairs. Outside she found a horse with reins, but without a saddle, grazing the dewy grass.

It was nearly dawn and she shivered, wishing that she had brought the white fur with her.

She led the horse over to a large stone and with some difficulty managed to mount.

Digging her heels into the horse's belly, she urged it forward. It jerked up and started for the archway.

There it unaccountably stopped. Rosaleena looked back. At a window, Geraldine stood staring down.

She could imagine the smile of disdain on her lips.

The horse moved on through the archway. Outside, it veered of its own accord towards a track to the left.

She made no attempt to check it. All she wanted was to put as much distance between herself and Bannaboy as possible.

The track descended through scree and rock and soon a mist enveloped herself and her mount.

After about an hour the mist lifted, but the terrain about her continued wild and uninhabited and she now felt drops of rain on her face and her heart sank. There was nowhere to shelter if the weather turn foul.

Another hour and she began to almost wish that she had not set out at all.

It was then she saw a row of thatched roofs in a vale beneath her. With renewed hope, she turned her horse towards them.

The hamlet boasted one muddy street, along which hens roamed at will. Over a door, a sign indicated that one of the shacks posed as a tavern and dusty bottles of ale stood jumbled in its window.

Rosaleena reined in her horse and, shaking her wet hair from her face, looked around.

A door creaked open and a man emerged from the shack to her left.

"Are you lost, ma'am?" he asked, casting a curious eye over her.

"As a matter of fact I am," replied Rosaleena.

"Will you no come in and dry yourself by the fire? My wife'll give you a bite of something hot to eat."

Rosaleena accepted gratefully and the man helped her from her horse and led her into his home.

It was comprised of one room with a ladder leading up to a loft. Rosaleena was pleasantly surprised to see how snug it was, despite the lack of luxury.

Over a crackling fire swung a black pot and the floor was covered in straw.

A woman rose from a chair before the hearth.

"This is my wife," said the man. "And I am the man of the house, Willy Hanlon by name."

"I am very pleased to meet you both. My name is – Rosaleena."

An enquiring look crossed Willy's features, but his wife was already at the black pot.

"Sit yourself in that chair there, miss," she ordered over her shoulder. "Sure, you're wet right through. Have you come far this morning?"

"I-I have been on the road since dawn," Rosaleena ventured. "I am not entirely sure where I am."

"You're in Crossmainham," answered Willy.

"I am lucky to have found you and Mrs. Hanlon at home," commented Rosaleena.

"Indeed you are," said Mrs. Hanlon, handing her a plate of porridge, "especially as the weather is worsening."

Rosaleena could hear torrents of rain falling.

"Do you think it will last very long?" she enquired anxiously as she took the plate. "I must get home today."

"And where is home?" Willy asked.

Rosaleena hesitated looking from Willy to his wife.

"Rosscullen House," she replied finally, lifting her spoon. "Near Rosscullen village."

Willy Hanlon dropped his pipe, which broke in two on the floor and his wife turned to stare at Rosaleena.

"What name did you give me when you arrived?" asked Willy at last.

Rosaleena was apprehensive.

"R-Rosaleena."

Willy paled, while Mrs. Hanlon bowed her head as if in prayer.

"I always knew this would happen," she muttered. "You did wrong, Willy Hanlon, you did wrong. And now here's the chance to put it right."

Rosaleena looked from one to the other in alarm.

"W-what do you mean, Mrs. Hanlon?" she asked.

Mrs. Hanlon gestured towards her husband.

"Ask that fellow. He's the one to tell you."

Willy rubbed his hand across his mouth.

"There's shame on me, miss," he said awkwardly. "And if anyone has a right to hear why, 'tis yourself. What you'll do with the knowledge, I daren't think."

Rosaleena waited expectantly.

"'Tis like this," Willy began. "Many years ago I was offered a 'tidy sum' to go along with three or four other men and attack a fellow, a big landlord, to give him a fright and get him to be more lenient-like with his tenants. I agreed to this and then, to my shame, discovered that the landlord in question was a certain Lord Rosscullen."

He paused, his eyes on Rosaleena.

She sat deathly still.

"The young Lord Rosscullen was not your usual class of a landlord," continued Willy. "He was known to help many a tenant who fell into arrears. I tried to pull out of the – conspiracy – but the other men wouldn't have it. I suppose they were afraid I'd squeal if I wasn't actively involved.

"So I went along with them and sure enough, all we did was make a lot of noise and threaten to break a few heads. We were beaten off anyways and no harm done on that occasion."

He paused, looking increasingly miserable.

"I was surprised a few months later," he resumed, "when I was asked to repeat the exercise. I was uneasy about it, but was offered a sum I couldn't refuse, for I had a baby on the way by then. There were more of us hired this time. The attack took place in some woods."

"The Magully Woods," intoned Rosaleena quietly.

Willy threw her a look.

"That's right. Well, at first it all seemed to go as before. Then, so sudden that I hadn't a hare's chance of intervenin', a shot rang out and – Rosscullen fell to the ground."

"W-who fired that shot?" asked Rosaleena. Now she would hear it – the name of the Earl, proving beyond all doubt that he was the murderer of her father.

"Why," said Willy, "Lord Rosscullen's companion. An Englishman I later learned was called Sir Uriel Reece."

Rosaleena leapt up, knocking over her chair.

"No – no – it was the Earl of Kilvarra. Tell me it was the Earl."

She was trembling in every limb and Mrs. Hanlon moved to take her in her arms.

"Wisht, now, wisht. My Willy was there and he's tellin' you what he saw."

Willy watched Rosaleena uneasily as he continued,

"I was never so disturbed in my life. This same Sir Reece, after firin' the shot, then leapt from his horse and ran off into the woods callin' 'murder, murder'.

"Thinkin' he meant to implicate ourselves, we beat a hasty retreat. But not before I picked up the musket that fired the fatal shot and thrust it into my saddlebag."

Mrs. Hanlon now took the story up.

"That Sir Reece claimed it was the Earl. And the Captain of the patrol that returned to the scene with him said it was the Earl, but sure that Captain was as dishonest a man as ever lived."

"W-what was *his* name?" asked Rosaleena faintly, sinking out of Mrs. Hanlon's embrace and into the chair.

"Huggins," said Willy Hanlon. "I saw him and Sir Reece talkin' together in a tavern soon after and Sir Reece handed Captain Huggins a bulgin' purse, the same kind of purse as he handed to us men when he hired us to carry out the first fake attack."

Rosaleena could barely speak.

"It was Sir Uriel who hired you?"

"He did," Willy growled. "But he hardly spoke to us at the time he hired us, only gruffly and under his breath, so I didn't realise he was English. If I had, I'd have been suspicious. So why would one Englishman want to frighten another? I thought – Heaven forgive me – that we were being asked to partake of a little political fun.

"I realise now it was a set-up for murder, in which the Earl would appear the guilty party. The Captain and his patrol were paid by Sir Reece to be nearby, in order to arrest the Earl when they found him at the scene."

Rosaleena now felt sick as she remembered Bridie – Geraldine – telling her that it was the Earl of Kilvarra who had come across her father's body.

Geraldine – and the Earl – had been telling the truth all along.

"Why then did you not speak up?" she demanded, venting her sudden anger with herself on Willy. "Why did you never exonerate the Earl?"

Willy gave a bitter guffaw.

"An Irishman attempt to exonerate an Irishman and against the word of an English gentleman and an English Militia Captain? And me with – political views that were well known. How would I have explained my participation at all? I might well have considered riskin' my neck if the Earl's neck were in danger.

"But he escaped and went to France and I hope he made his fortune there. I never took money for that second attack. So I left the area and settled here in Crossmainham with my wife and baby, though the boy, alas, died and we never had another.

"The guilt was always on me that I had anythin' to do with that Sir Reece, for Rosscullen was a fine man and a good landlord to all."

Rosaleena's mind was racing.

"You said you took the murder weapon from the scene?"

"I did," confirmed Willy. "I have it yet."

Rosaleena gulped.

"May I – see it?"

Without a word, Willy gestured to his wife. Mrs. Hanlon opened the lid of the settle and drew out a bundle wrapped in oilskin.

She carried it over to Willy. He took it from her and, unwrapping it, revealed a well-polished black musket.

Rosaleena took the musket in trepidation. Barely was it in her hands than she burst into tears.

"I never thought," she sobbed, "to hold the weapon that killed my father."

Willy hung his head.

"I guessed it right enough. You have his look about you."

He pointed at the musket.

"Do you see Sir Uriel Reece's initials inscribed there on the barrel?"

Through her tears, Rosaleena examined the musket and gave a nod.

"I'd say that was evidence of his guilt," said Willy Hanlon with satisfaction.

His wife gave a snort.

"And what then are you goin' to do about it, Willy Hanlon? With the poor victim's daughter standin' there before you. What are you goin' to do after all this time?"

"Why," said Willy, amazed. "What should I do?"

Rosaleena replied, wiping her wet cheeks.

"You will go with me to McEvoy, the lawyer who handles the Rosscullen estate and repeat your story and we will take the musket with us too. Mr. McEvoy will surely believe an Irishman – if that man is in the company of the murdered man's daughter!"

Willy Hanlon hesitated, regarding Rosaleena from under lowered brows.

It was Mrs. Hanlon who made the decision.

"He'll go with you, miss," she said. "He'll go with you or I'll make his life a misery till the end of his days!"

# CHAPTER TEN

Willy owned a cart, which was usually pulled by a forlorn looking donkey, but for the sake of speed, he set Rosaleena's horse into the shafts.

Just before midday they set off.

Mr. McEvoy was just finishing lunch when the two arrived at his house.

He stood amazed when he learned who Rosaleena was and he listened carefully to her tale.

"I am shocked," he said when she ended, shaking his head in disbelief. "Shocked beyond measure."

He turned to Willy.

"Where is this musket she speaks of?"

Willy took the musket from under his coat and then pushed it across the table.

Mr. McEvoy examined the item closely, noting the initials inscribed on the barrel. Finally he laid it down and turned to Rosaleena with a sigh,

"This will be a terrible blow to your mother. She sets great store by her step-brother as you well know."

"Only because he made himself so indispensable to her after my poor father's death," replied Rosaleena. "Mr. McEvoy, did you never suspect my uncle?"

Mr. McEvoy shook his head.

"Of murder, no. But of opportunism, yes. Why, his first move on arriving at Rosscullen House was to try and borrow money from your father."

Rosaleena expressed her surprise and Mr. McEvoy regarded her gravely.

"Apparently Sir Uriel needed ready cash for one of his business schemes. I counselled your father against such a loan and he took my advice. Imagine, then, my surprise when he turned up to make a will with Sir Uriel in tow.

"And I was even more surprised when Sir Uriel was named as Guardian and Trustee and I could only think that your father was deeply grateful for his help in fighting off those first assailants. After your father's death I could not help but notice the alacrity with which Sir Uriel assumed his duties with regard to your mother and yourself."

"He controlled our lives," said Rosaleena in a low voice, "until I reached the age to come into my inheritance. At which point, sooner than relinquish control, he planned to marry me off to his own son! Only the Earl guessed the truth – only the Earl came to rescue me from my fate!"

She turned her face away to hide her emotion.

Mr. McEvoy drummed his fingers on the table.

"It is the fate of the Earl that now concerns me, Rosaleena. Following your 'kidnap', Sir Uriel, Oswald and Captain Huggins have been hunting him in league with a certain suspect section of the Militia. From what you have now told me, I am certain that they mean to kill the Earl rather than bring him in alive.

"Alive and in Ireland he is a threat to the guilty, as he was not when abroad during the French Wars."

Rosaleena was distraught.

She begged Mr. McEvoy to send someone to warn the Earl that he must on no account give himself up to Sir Uriel and his party should they find him. She also begged him to arrange for the arrest of Sir Uriel.

Mr. McEvoy assured her that he intended to do as she wished, but it would take a little time to organise.

Rosaleena said that she would leave for Bannaboy Tower immediately to warn the Earl herself.

"I must absolutely forbid that," said Mr. McEvoy. "The matter is now best placed in the hands of the law."

Willy agreed with the lawyer.

"Why don't you just wait here and rest, miss?" he suggested to Rosaleena. "I'll go with Mr. McEvoy to rustle up some men we can trust."

Rosaleena, sensing their determination not to let her go to the Earl alone, thought quickly. She gave a nod of acquiescence and then sank into a chair by the fire.

She waited for the closing of the front door behind the two men before she rose swiftly.

Taking the musket from where it lay on the table, she tiptoed out of the house.

The horse and cart were on the front railings and Rosaleena climbed swiftly into the cart and lifted the reins.

She knew the way back to Crossmainham village and from there Mrs. Hanlon would surely help her retrace the route to Bannaboy Tower.

Her mind had only one aim.

The Earl had saved her from falling into the trap of marrying Oswald.

Now she must save him.

She drove the cart at a great rate, mud flying out from under its wheels. She was at Crossmainham in less than the two hours it had taken to travel from there.

Barely had she stopped outside the Hanlons' house when the door flew open and Mrs. Hanlon appeared.

"Get out of here, quick," hissed Mrs. Hanlon. "Sir Uriel and his party are over at the inn. They stopped off in Crossmainham to cajole Willy into joinin' them, but I was able to say he was not at home. Go on with you, go, before they see you!"

Trembling, Rosaleena lifted up the reins to drive on, but she was too late. The door of the inn opened and men began to stream into the road and among them were Captain Huggins, Oswald and Sir Uriel.

Catching sight of Rosaleena in the trap, Sir Uriel stood rigid.

"It's Rosaleena," gasped Oswald.

"So I see," muttered Sir Uriel.

He walked to the cart and took hold of the reins, staring up at Rosaleena.

"Why, niece," he said, "we were afraid you were murdered – or worse."

Rosaleena regarded him calmly.

"As you see, Uncle, I am alive and unharmed. The Earl – released me."

"Just like that?"

"Just like that. So – there's no reason to go after him now, is there?"

Her uncle turned with a jeer to his companions.

"Do you hear that, gentlemen? My niece says we can all go home!"

Rosaleena reddened as they roared with laughter.

Sir Uriel turned back to his niece.

"We were hunting for the Earl of Kilvarra before he kidnapped you, and we will go on hunting him until we have him by the neck."

Rosaleena shivered at his words.

Oswald then tugged at his father's elbow.

"Papa, why don't I escort Rosaleena home?"

He looked bedraggled and sorry for himself and she guessed that he had little appetite in hunting down the Earl.

Sir Uriel brushed his son away.

"No. This meeting with your cousin is opportune. Rosaleena will be able to lead us to the place where she was held and so save us a great deal of trouble. We have already ridden to Kilvarra and we know that she was not held there."

Rosaleena swallowed.

"The mist was very thick when I escaped, Uncle. I cannot be sure of the way."

"But you will try?"

Rosaleena steeled herself to reply,

"Of course, Uncle."

Sir Uriel ordered Oswald to ride with Rosaleena. He mounted the cart and sat beside her.

She had already decided that she was going to lead the company completely astray and if she could not get to the Earl herself to warn him, she could at least keep them at bay until Mr. McEvoy and Willy made it to Bannaboy.

Sir Uriel rode at the side of the cart. She began her deception by directing the party right past the track which she had followed to come down into Crossmainham.

A mile out of the village she signalled that the party should turn North and Sir Uriel signalled them to rein in.

"North? Are you sure?" he asked menacingly.

"As I say, Uncle, it was very misty."

He leaned down and caught a handful of her hair.

"I think you are trying to save the neck of that mad Irishman," he snarled.

She wrenched her head away from his grip.

"No, Uncle, I-I'm not."

"Papa, there's something carved on a stone by the road," Oswald now piped up

"What does it say, boy?"

"It says 'Bannaboy'," called out Captain Huggins. "There's an arrow pointing up the mountainside."

A cold smile stole across Sir Uriel's features as he watched Rosaleena struggle to disguise her alarm.

"Bannaboy, indeed? Let's ride that way then."

"It would a waste of time," said Rosaleena quickly. "I did not ride downhill when I escaped, I am sure."

Sir Uriel ignored her.

Then, turning up the track indicated by the stone, he beckoned his men on.

Rosaleena felt wretched. All she could hope was that the Earl had left Bannaboy after she had escaped.

It was a full hour's ride before Bannaboy appeared ahead. The tower seemed so deserted as the party rode in that Rosaleena's spirits rose.

But, as Sir Uriel dismounted, the door of the tower opened and the Earl stepped out.

His gaze swept so coldly over Rosaleena that it was obvious he suspected that she had led his enemies to him.

She almost wept to see him there, so tall and proud, the breeze ruffling his dark hair, his eyes full of defiance.

"I was not expecting to see you here so soon," he said to Sir Uriel.

"Nevertheless," sneered Sir Uriel, "here we are, the representatives of the law and we will expect you to submit without a struggle."

"Expecting it, are you?" asked the Earl coolly. "It's my feeling that only a guilty man would agree to do so."

"You *are* a guilty man," cried Sir Uriel. "You will submit to the law now as you should have submitted to it twenty-one years ago."

"And twenty-one years ago you were a villain," growled the Earl, "and it seems you still are!"

"There are ten of us here," Captain Huggins called out threateningly. "You'll not escape justice."

The Earl shrugged.

"Ten of you, perhaps, but I think you will agree that I have the advantage?"

He gestured at the first story of the tower, where his sister and cousins were now visible at the windows with muskets trained on Sir Uriel and his companions.

Captain Huggins gave a snort.

"You'd shed more innocent blood, Kilvarra?"

The Earl regarded the Captain with distaste.

"I have never shed innocent blood," he said. "Nor have I conspired to accuse an innocent man of murder."

"If you didn't murder Rosscullen," said the Captain icily, "then who did?"

It was now that Rosaleena, finding her courage at last, decided to speak out.

"I have something here," she began, but before she could go on Oswald clamped his hand over her mouth.

"I don't trust you!" he hissed. "One more word and your Irishman is dead."

Rosaleena gave out a cry as she saw that in his free hand Oswald held a musket, which was trained directly on the Earl.

The Earl swung round at the sound of the exchange. His pupils flared at what he saw.

"Unhand that lady," he growled.

Oswald's lips curled.

"Why should you concern yourself with someone who betrayed you and led us all to your hideout?"

She struggled in dismay at this lie, but Oswald's hand was firm.

"Anyway," he continued, "she's now as good as my wife. Mine to do as I please with. And as soon as the ring's on her finger, *I will!*"

Rosaleena heard the Earl give a curse.

Fearful that he would do something rash, she made one last attempt to free herself of Oswald's grasp, twisting her head back and sinking her teeth onto his thumb.

With a shriek he drew his hand away.

Determined to show that she had proof of the Earl's innocence, Rosaleena quickly reached for Sir Uriel's old musket that she had concealed under her cloak.

Oswald, seeing it, lunged to take it from her.

She resisted. The two of them swayed a moment in a deadly tussle before a shot rang out in the clear cold air.

The horse pulling Willy's cart reared in alarm and Rosaleena was sent spinning through the air.

She knew no more.

*

Rosaleena opened her eyes to see firelight dancing on a ceiling.

She raised her head slowly and saw that she was in her own room at Rosscullen House, although how she had come there she had no idea.

Her mother rose from a chair by the fire and hurried anxiously to the bedside.

"How are you, my dear?"

Rosaleena's hand strayed to her forehead where her fingers encountered a bandage.

"What happened to me?"

Lady Rosscullen sighed.

"You were thrown violently headfirst against a tree. You have been concussed for several days."

"I-I was not shot?"

Lady Rosscullen shuddered.

"No, dear, you were not shot."

"Then – who was?" she asked in a small voice.

Her mother seemed unable to speak and Rosaleena started up in unguarded dismay.

"The Earl? Was it the Earl, Mama?"

Lady Rosscullen gave a reluctant nod.

"In your struggle with Oswald, the musket went off and the Earl was hit."

Rosaleena fell back weak with terror.

"Was he – killed?"

"I am told he was carried into the tower severely wounded. His sister would allow no one to attend him but herself."

"What have you heard of him since?"

Lady Rosscullen hesitated.

"The incident occurred five days ago," she said at length. "Nothing has been heard of him since."

Rosaleena closed her eyes, lips trembling.

"Who brought me home? Uncle Uriel?"

"It was Mr. McEvoy."

Having said this, Lady Rosscullen suddenly knelt at the bedside and took her daughter's hand in hers.

"Rosaleena – your uncle is dead."

Rosaleena's eyes flew open.

"Dead?" she echoed. "H-how?"

"Just as the Earl fell, the lawyer McEvoy arrived on the scene with Willy Hanlon and some of the Rosscullen

Militia. Resisting arrest, Sir Uriel drew his musket and was shot in the chest – by one of the Militia men. Captain Huggins and his accomplices threw down their weapons."

Lady Rosscullen began to weep as she recounted the facts and Rosaleena tried to console her mother.

"I am so sorry, Mama. I know how fond you were of – of your step-brother."

"Fond?" echoed Lady Rosscullen bitterly. "It was only when I heard that he was dead that I realised I had been afraid of him all my life. He was always a bully and now I have learned that he was a villain too."

"So you know all?" said Rosaleena softly.

"Mr. McEvoy enlightened me." Her mother let out a sudden wail. "Oh, Rosaleena, what a fool I have been! Allowing my husband's killer to take over our lives."

"You were not to know, Mama, that Sir Uriel was a dissembler."

"Indeed he was. You haven't asked about Oswald, my dear."

Rosaleena stared at the ceiling.

"How is he?"

"As you can imagine, he was devastated to learn the truth about his father. He and I both hope it will not – prejudice you against his suit."

Rosaleena turned her head to stare at her mother.

"Mama, you surely cannot think I would marry him after all that has happened?"

"You cannot blame the son for the character of his father! Whatever you feel for the Earl, you were promised to Oswald and, if the Earl had not interfered, you would be his wife now. To go ahead with the marriage would heal the terrible wound our family has endured."

Rosaleena felt a curious weariness as she heard her mother out. It was obvious that Oswald had been pleading his case with Lady Rosscullen just as his father had done.

It was now clear that she had succumbed, taking as she always did the line of least resistance.

Her mother rose as a knock came on the door.

"I believe this is Oswald. Shall I allow him in?"

Rosaleena nodded numbly and her mother ushered Oswald in and then withdrew.

Oswald moved awkwardly to the foot of the bed, where he stood picking at the wood of the bedpost.

Rosaleena watched him through narrowed eyes as she was remembering how Oswald had lied to the Earl, accusing her of leading Sir Uriel and his men to Bannaboy.

At the same time he looked so thin and woebegone that she almost felt a little sorry for him. He had always been under the thumb of his father.

What a shock to learn that he was a murderer!

Oswald apologised for his behaviour at Bannaboy, insisting that it was due to jealousy. He had believed that she wanted to help the Earl because she was in love with him.

"I did not realise," he said, "that it was because you knew and cared for the truth."

Rosaleena remained silent. She did not feel inclined to correct him about her motives for helping the Earl.

"I don't suppose," Oswald ventured awkwardly, "I don't suppose there's a chance of you marrying me now?"

Rosaleena lay still.

"I don't even want to consider the matter now," she murmured truthfully.

He appeared to take this as a cause for optimism. After a little more talk he then went away almost satisfied, leaving Rosaleena to ponder her fate.

The musket that she had carried to Bannaboy, the very musket that had killed her father, might well now be responsible for the death of the man she loved.

She did not know if the Earl was alive or dead.

Tears welled in her eyes as she faced the fact that, if alive, he was certainly making no effort to contact her.

For all she knew, he might even believe that she had intended to shoot him.

Whatever else, he could surely never forgive her for her lack of faith in him and for what he would perceive as her treachery in guiding Sir Uriel to his hideout.

She had acted foolishly in trying to reach Bannaboy and the Earl before anyone else she was ready to admit.

Truly, she deserved no better than to marry Oswald.

'He would be my penance,' she thought glumly.

*

The next morning at breakfast she was disappointed to learn that both Mary and Mrs. Lynch had left.

Recalling Mrs. Lynch's role in releasing 'Bridie' from the cellar, she tentatively asked her mother whether the housekeeper had been dismissed.

"No, she was not," said her mother curtly. "Both she and Mary suddenly found employment elsewhere."

Rosaleena was downcast. The departure of the two employees left her with no one in the household who might be able to bring her news of the Earl.

The only other person who might have relieved her anguish was Mr McEvoy, but, when she asked after him, her mother informed her that he was away in London.

The doctor arrived soon after breakfast to remove Rosaleena's bandage. The cut she had suffered had healed. All that was left was a small scar that would fade in time.

She was to all intents and purposes recovered. He was, however, disturbed by her low spirits and privately suggested to Lady Rosscullen that she needed a companion of some sort.

"She has Oswald," her mother replied petulantly.

*

The days passed by without incident and Rosaleena grew increasingly despondent.

Soon she found herself almost welcoming Oswald's company. At least he was someone to play cards with.

After a while the very fact of his presence began to act on her resolve like the drip, drip of water on stone.

She wondered if he felt as lost as she. Perhaps he wanted to marry her because he could think of nothing else to do with his life.

Certainly she had to admit that she could think of nothing else to do with *her* life.

At last, caring little for her future since it did not include the Earl, Rosaleena agreed once again to marry her step-cousin.

There was little fanfare.

*

On the morning of the wedding Rosaleena's new maid dressed her for the Church.

A distant relation of her father's, a Mr. White, had been summoned to give her away and after her mother had gone to the Church, this gentleman drove up in his carriage to escort Rosaleena.

She had first met Mr. White the day before and was surprised when he merely tipped his hat at her and turned his attention back to his horses. It was strange indeed that he had decided to drive the carriage himself.

She then climbed into the carriage, wondering at its modest proportions.

Her mother had assured her that Mr. White was a man of no mean fortune.

She leaned back on the somewhat worn upholstery and closed her eyes.

She had not seen Oswald for two days. He had suddenly decided to take himself off to await the marriage elsewhere, claiming it was unlucky to remain in the same house as his bride-to-be.

She opened her eyes as the carriage began to shake and rattle with such ferocity that she realised it must have left the road.

Looking out, she saw that it was travelling over a rough track through a forest of pines.

Pulling the window down, she then called up to Mr. White that he had taken the wrong turn, but he affected not to hear her.

A few minutes later her heart gave a strange lurch as the carriage rolled to a halt in a clearing she recognised.

Opening the carriage door, she heard the sound of a waterfall in her ears and felt its spray on her cheeks.

All thought now of her mother and Oswald and the Church where they waited for her vanished from her mind.

Trembling, she climbed down.

She looked up at the driver's box and saw not Mr. White regarding her but Willy Hanlon!

Acknowledging her with a smile, Willy gestured towards the pool.

"There's another friend of yours," he said.

Turning, Rosaleena saw Mrs. Lynch. With a cry of pleasure, she ran towards the old lady's embrace.

"Mrs. Lynch! Tell me, oh, do tell me, for you must surely know. Does the Earl live or am I indeed responsible for his death?" she asked breathlessly.

"He lives," came a voice and Rosaleena whirled round to find the Earl standing in front of her!

"Yes, he surely lives," the Earl repeated. "Though, Rosaleena, you did your best to silence him, for your bullet grazed his heart. A heart you had already wounded."

Rosaleena could not speak for joy.

The Earl's gaze travelled questioningly to her dress and her countenance fell.

"I am to be m-married," she cried forlornly.

"I know it," replied the Earl.

"Y-you do?"

"I do. And having rescued you from the procedure once, I feel disinclined to rescue you again."

"Oh," said Rosaleena faintly.

"In fact," continued the Earl, "I mean to force you to marry, whatever."

Tears filled Rosaleena's eyes.

Had she been brought here so that the Earl might take the opportunity of humiliating her?

"Y-you are right to make me – fulfil my duty," she intoned miserably.

"I am glad you see it as your duty," approved the Earl. "For the Priest is here, the witnesses are here and, most of all, the bride is here. What more is wanting?"

Rosaleena's eyes now widened as Mr. McEvoy and Mary emerged from the shadows to stand with Mrs. Lynch and Willy, while a Priest with his breviary appeared by the pool.

The Earl smiled at her dawning comprehension.

"Mr. McEvoy told me of your brave efforts to help me, Rosaleena. In the circumstances I am determined that you will marry me."

"H-here?" stammered Rosaleena.

"In the Rosscullen Chapel, here by the pool," the Earl indicated. "It has never been deconsecrated and will suit our purpose. Mr. McEvoy has seen to all the legal niceties."

Faint with longing to be his, Rosaleena nevertheless felt that she had to remind him that she was not free. At this very moment, Oswald waited at the altar for her. How could she break his heart a second time?

The Earl threw back his head with a huge roar of laughter.

"You will not be breaking his heart at all, only his expectations. He could not envisage any other future for himself but you, until Mr. McEvoy returned from business he had in London with a message.

"The message was from your good friend, Lalage, and was of a tenor that encouraged the young Mr. Reece to believe that he had the good chance of capturing *her* heart and thus *her* fortune, which happens to be far greater than your own."

Rosaleena swallowed, thinking of how Oswald had decided not to remain at Rosscullen for the few days prior to their wedding.

"And has he gone to her and is not waiting for me at the Church?"

"He has gone to her," replied the Earl gently. "So you are free to accept my hand, which, since my innocence has been proved and my fortunes restored, I consider I am free to offer."

Rosaleena burst into tears.

"B-but my mother!"

The Earl took her face in his hands.

"Mr. McEvoy will inform your mother of what has transpired. Once she learns of Oswald Reece's perfidy, she will be as happy as yourself to have you married – even if it is to a feckless Irishman."

There was one last question.

"And – Mr. White? What happened to him?"

"Willy spent all last evening in the tavern with him. Mr. White is still sleeping off the effects!"

So it was there, in the little Chapel by the waterfall, that Rosaleena and the Earl were married with Geraldine and Mary acting as bridesmaids and Mrs. Lynch, Willy and Mr. McEvoy as witnesses.

Rosaleena was overjoyed to hear that Mrs. Lynch and Mary were now employed by the Earl, while Willy was to be his coachman.

The ceremony done, the Priest and the witnesses departed, the Earl then scooped up his bride and carried her through the pool to the cave.

"My hunger for you is too great," he murmured into her ear. "I must claim you here and now or die!"

Once within the cave, Rosaleena was amazed.

It had become a bridal chamber. A wide bed stood at its centre strewn with white furs and red roses.

On a long table, lit by four shining candelabra, lay platters of food and silver goblets for wine.

The Earl lay Rosaleena tenderly down on the white furs and, turning her head, she felt their softness against her cheek.

The Earl threw off his cloak and knelt above her.

Eyes dark with desire, he loosened his white shirt. Falling open, it revealed his broad chest and the scar that lay above his heart.

Rosaleena murmured in horror.

"Did I do that?"

"You did. And now I demand my recompense."

"How shall I pay you?" she asked tremulously.

"With your heart, your soul and your body," replied the Earl huskily, reaching to unlace her gown.

Rosaleena checked him.

"Those other matters – that kept you in France after the war!" she reminded him.

The Earl bent low.

Lips close to her ear, he told her that she should not resent the experience he gained in France that would now carry her to such heights of rapture that she could never even have imagined.

"But you alone are capable of arousing me beyond all reason," he reassured her. "You alone can ignite this fire of passion that rages through my whole being!"

Rosaleena moaned as she listened to his words.

Her heart ached for him.

God had graciously heard all her prayers and had answered them and was blessing her love for the Earl and his love for her.

She shook as he drew aside her gown and gazed upon her pure pale beauty.

Together then they plunged into that wilder kind of love so long promised and yet so long denied, a love that brought her trembling to the very Gates of Heaven.